**Every instinct Daisy possessed railed against it. She hated the idea! But what was the alternative? If she told Sariq, then what? He'd be devastated.**

She knew what was at stake for him, and why he needed to marry one of the women who would help him keep the peace in his country. The fact she'd fallen pregnant wasn't his fault and he didn't deserve to have to deal with this complication. More important, he wouldn't want to deal with it. He'd made that perfectly clear during their time together. It had been a brief passionate affair, nothing more. He'd gone back to the RKH and moved on with his life—the last thing he'd be expecting was the news that, actually, they'd made a baby together.

But didn't he have a right to know? This was his child. When she stripped away the fact he was a powerful sheikh, he was a man who had the same biological claim on this developing baby as she did.

**Clare Connelly** was raised in small-town Australia among a family of avid readers. She spent much of her childhood up a tree, Harlequin romance book in hand. Clare is married to her own real-life hero and they live in a bungalow near the sea with their two children. She is frequently found staring into space—a surefire sign she is in the world of her characters. She has a penchant for French food and ice-cold champagne, and Harlequin novels continue to be her favorite-ever books. Writing for Harlequin Presents is a long-held dream. Clare can be contacted via clareconnelly.com or on her Facebook page.

## Books by Clare Connelly

### Harlequin Presents

*Bought for the Billionaire's Revenge*
*Innocent in the Billionaire's Bed*
*Her Wedding Night Surrender*
*Bound by the Billionaire's Vows*
*Spaniard's Baby of Revenge*
*Redemption of the Untamed Italian*

### Secret Heirs of Billionaires

*Shock Heir for the King*

### Christmas Seductions

*Bound by Their Christmas Baby*
*The Season to Sin*

### Crazy Rich Greek Weddings

*The Greek's Billion-Dollar Baby*
*Bride Behind the Billion-Dollar Veil*

Visit the Author Profile page
at Harlequin.com for more titles.

# Clare Connelly

---

## THE SECRET KEPT FROM THE KING

**HARLEQUIN**
# PRESENTS

ISBN-13: 978-1-335-89365-9

The Secret Kept from the King

Harlequin Enterprises ULC
22 Adelaide St. West, 40th Floor
Toronto, Ontario M5H 4E3, Canada
www.Harlequin.com

**Printed in U.S.A.**

# THE SECRET KEPT
# FROM THE KING

This book's for you—a romance reader who, just like me, loves to be swept up in a passionate, escapist story with a guaranteed happily-ever-after.

# CHAPTER ONE

WHEN HE CLOSED his eyes he saw only his father's, so he tried not to close them much at all. Not because he didn't want to see the Exalted Sheikh Kadir Al Antarah again; he did, more than anything. But seeing his eyes as they'd been at the end, so clouded by pain and unconscious of the world that swirled around him, so robbed of the strength and vibrancy that had been hallmarks of his life and rule, made Sariq's chest compress in a way that robbed him of breath and had him gasping for air.

The King was dead. His father was dead. He was now completely alone in this world, and the inescapable reality he had been aware of all his life was wrapping around him like a cable.

He had been crowned. The job of steering the Royal Kingdom of Haleth fell to him. Just as he'd always known it would, just as he'd spent a lifetime preparing for.

'Your Highness? Malik has asked me to remind you of the time.'

Sariq didn't respond at first. He continued to stare out at the glittering vista of Manhattan. From this vantage point, it was easy to pick out the key buildings that were considered the most well-known landmarks of New York. The Empire State building shone like a beacon. The Chrysler with its art deco detailing, and, far in the distance, the spire of One World Trade Centre. And in another direction, not far from this hotel, if he followed a straight line, he'd reach the United Nations, where he'd be expected to make his first official speech since the death of Sheikh Kadir. In the morning, he'd address leaders and delegates from dozens of countries, aiming to assure them that his father's death was not an end to the peace that had, finally, been established between the RKH and the west.

'Emir?'

'Yes.' He spoke more harshly than he'd intended. He closed his eyes—and there was his father. He returned his attention to the view, his features locked in a grim mask. 'Tell Malik I am aware of the hour.'

Still, the servant hovered. 'Can I get you anything else, sir?'

Briefly, Sariq turned to face the servant. He

was little more than a boy—sixteen or seventeen perhaps. He wore the same uniform Sariq had donned at that age, black with gold detailing. The insignia indicated he was an ensign. 'What is your name?'

The boy's eyes widened.

'Kaleth.'

Sariq forced a smile to his face. It felt odd, heavy and wooden. 'Thank you for your attention, Kaleth, but you may go now.'

Kaleth paused, as though he wished to say something further.

'Tell Malik it was at my insistence.'

This seemed to appease the young officer because he nodded and bowed low. 'Goodnight, sir.'

He turned back to the view without responding. It was after midnight and his day had been long. Starting with meetings in Washington and then the flight to New York, where he'd had dinner with his ambassador to America—also installed in this hotel while the major renovations to the embassy were completed. And all day long, he'd pushed his grief aside, knowing he needed to act strong and unaffected by the fact he'd buried his father a little over three weeks ago.

The man had been a behemoth. Strength personified. His absence left a gaping hole—not just for Sariq but for the country. It was one

Sariq would endeavour to fill, but there would only ever be one King Kadir.

He moved towards the view, pushing one of the sliding glass doors open so he could step onto the large, private terrace, his eyes continuing to trace the skyline of New York. The background noise of horns beeping, sirens wailing and engines revving was a constant here, and somehow that made it fade into nothing. It was so loud it became a sort of white noise, and yet it made him long for the silence of the desert to the east of his palace, a place where he could erect a tent and be surrounded by silence, and the ancient sands of his kingdom. There was wisdom in those grains of sand: each and every one of them had stood sentinel to the people of his kingdom. Their wars, their famines, their pains, their hopes, their beliefs and, in the last forty years, their peace, their prosperity, their modernisation and acceptance onto the world's stage.

It was his father's legacy and Sariq would do all that he could to preserve it. No, not simply to preserve it: to improve it. To grow it, to strengthen it, to better his country's standing and make peace so unequivocal that the trailing fingers of civil war could no longer touch a single soul of his country.

Sariq was not his father, but he was of him, he was cast from his soul, his bones and strength, and he had spent a lifetime watching, learning, and preparing for this.

In the morning, it would begin. He was ready.

Daisy stared at the flashing light with a small frown on her cupid's bow lips, then consulted the clock on the wall. It was three in the morning, and the alarm for the Presidential suite was on. She reached for the phone, tucking it under her ear.

'Concierge, how may I help you?'

It had only been a matter of hours since the delegation from the Royal Kingdom of Haleth had been installed in this five-star hotel's most prestigious suite—as well as a whole floor of rooms for servants and security guards—but Daisy had already had multiple dealings with a man named Malik, who seemed to coordinate the life of the Sheikh. As the hotel's VIP concierge, this was her job—she alone was responsible for taking care of every little thing the most prestigious guests wanted. Whether it was organising parties for after their concerts at Madison Square Garden, or, in the case of a Queen from a Scandinavian country, organising a small couture fashion parade in her suite so she could choose what to wear to the Met gala, Daisy prided herself on being able to cope with just about anything that was asked of her.

So when the phone rang, despite the hour, she was calm and prepared. Malik must need something and she would ensure he got it.

What she wasn't prepared for was the timbre of the voice that came down the line, so deep and throaty, accented with spice and an exotic lilt that showed English was his second language. 'I would like some persimmon tea.'

The RKH ambassador had been staying in the hotel for three months while the embassy was being renovated. They now had a permanent supply of delicacies from that country on hand, including persimmon tea.

'Yes, sir. Would you like some *balajari* as well?' she offered, the almond and lemon zest biscuits something the ambassador always took with his tea.

There was a slight pause. 'Fine.' The call was disconnected and Daisy inwardly bristled, though she showed no sign of that. Very few of the guests she'd hosted in the Presidential suite had exhibited particularly good manners. There were a few exceptions: an Australian actor who'd apologised every time he'd 'disturbed' her, a Scottish woman who'd won one of those television singing competitions and seemed unable to comprehend that she'd been jettisoned in the global superstar arena and seemed to want to be treated as normally as possible, and a Jap-

anese artist who had wanted directions to the
nearest Whole Foods so she could stock her own
fridge.

Daisy called the order through to the kitchen
then moved to the service elevator. There was
a full-length mirror there—the hotel manager
insisted that each staff member check their appearance before going out on the floor, and
Daisy did so now, tucking a curl of her blonde
hair back into its bun, pinching her cheeks to
bring a bit of colour to them, and even though
her shirt was tucked in, she pushed it in a little more firmly, straightening her pencil skirt
and spinning to have a look over her shoulder
at her behind.

Neat, professional, nondescript. Her job
wasn't to be noticed, it was to fly beneath the
radar. She was a facilitator, and nothing more.
A ghost of the hotel, there whenever she was
required, but in an unseen kind of way.

By the time she reached the kitchen in the
basement, the order was ready. She double-
checked the tray herself, inspecting plates for
fingerprints, the teapot for heat, then thanked
the staff, carrying the tray on one hand as she
pressed the call button for the lift.

The Presidential suite was on the top floor
and only she and the hotel manager had a staff
access card for it. She swiped it as she entered

then moved the tray to both hands, holding it in front of her as the lift shot up towards the sky.

When she'd first started working here, two years ago, the elevator had made her tummy ache every time, but she was used to it now and barely batted an eyelid.

The doors pinged open into a small service corridor with a glossy white door on one end. In the presidential apartment, the door was concealed by wall panelling. She knocked discreetly and, despite the absence of a greeting, unlocked the door and pushed into the suite.

The lights were out but several lamps had been turned on, giving the apartment an almost eerie glow.

She loved these rooms, with their sumptuous décor, their stunning views, the promise of luxury and grandeur. Of course, she loved them most of all when they were empty, particularly of the more demanding and disrespectful guests who had a tendency to treat the delicate furniture as though it were cheap, plastic tat.

The coffee table in the middle of the sofas was low-set and a shining timber. She placed the tea tray down on it, then straightened to look around the room. At first, she didn't see him. It took her eyes a moment to adjust to the darkened room. But then, the silhouette of a man stood out, a void against the Manhattan skyline.

The Sheikh.

She'd caught a glimpse of him at a distance, earlier that day, and he was instantly recognisable now. It wasn't just his frame, which was tall and broad, muscled in a way that spoke of fitness and strength. It was his long hair, dark, which he wore in a bun on top of his head. She was used to dealing with powerful, important people and yet that didn't mean she was an automaton. In moments like this, a hint of anxiety always bristled through her. She ignored it, keeping her voice neutral when she addressed him.

'Good evening, sir. I have your tea.' A pause, in which he didn't speak, nor did he turn to face her. 'Would you like me to pour it for you?'

Another pause, a silence that stretched between them for several seconds. She waited with the appearance of impassivity, watching him, so she saw the moment he dipped his head forward in what she took to be a nod.

Her fingertips trembled betrayingly as she reached for the teapot, lifting it silently, pressing down on the lid to avoid any spills, filling the tea to near the top of the cup, then silently replacing the pot on the tray.

She took a step backward then, preparing to leave. Except he still didn't move and something inside her sparked with curiosity. Not just cu-

riosity: ~~duty. He had asked for tea; her job was~~
to provide him with it. She moved back to the
coffee table, lifting the teacup and saucer, carrying them across the room towards him.

'Here you are, sir,' she murmured at his side.
Now, finally, he did turn to look at her, and she
had to grip the teacup and saucer more tightly
to stop them from shaking. Her fingers felt as
though they'd been filled with jelly. She'd seen
him from a distance and she'd seen photographs
of him, when she'd been preparing for his visit,
but nothing really did justice to his magnifi-
cence. In person, he was so much more vital
than any still image could convey. His features
were harsh, symmetrical and almost jagged. A
jaw that was square, cheekbones that appeared
to have been slashed into his face at birth, a
nose that had a bump halfway down its length,
as if it had been broken at some point. His eyes
were the darkest black, and his brows were thick
and straight. His skin was a swarthy tan, and
his chin was covered in stubble. Yes, up close
he was quite mesmerising, so she forced herself
to look away. Being mesmerised wasn't part of
her job description.

'It's supposed to help you sleep.' His voice
was unlike anything she'd ever known. If you
could find a way to bottle it, you'd be a mil-
lionaire.

'I've heard that.' She nodded, crisply, already preparing to fade into the background, to disappear discreetly through the concealed doorway, feeling almost as though her disappearing now was essential to her sanity.

'Have you tried it before?'

'No.' She swallowed; her throat felt quite dry. 'But your ambassador favours it.'

'It is very common in my country.'

His eyes roamed her face in a way that set her pulse firing. Escape was essential. 'Do you need anything else?'

A small frown quirked at his lips. He looked back towards the view. 'Malik would say I need to sleep.'

'And you have the tea for that.'

'Scotch might work better.'

'Would you like me to organise some for you?'

He tilted his head to hers again. 'It's after three.'

His words made little sense.

'It's after three and you're working.'

'Oh, right. Yes. That's my job.'

He lifted a brow. 'To work through the night?'

'To work when you need me,' she said with a lift of her shoulders. Then, with a swift correction, 'Or when any guest of the Presidential suite requires me. I'm assigned to this suite exclusively.'

'And you have to do whatever I ask?' he prompted.

A small smile lifted her lips. 'Well, not quite.' She couldn't suppress the teasing quality from her voice. 'I can't cook and I don't know any jokes, but when it comes to facilitating your requests, then yes, I do whatever is humanly possible to make them happen.'

'And that's your employment.'

'Yes.'

He sipped the tea without taking his dark eyes off her. Ordinarily, she would have taken that opportunity to leave, but there was a contradiction within this man that had her saying, 'I would have thought you'd be used to that degree of service.'

'Why do you say that?'

'Because you travel with an entourage of forty men, all of whom it would appear exist to serve your every whim?'

Another sip of his tea. 'Yes, this is their job. I am King, and in my country serving the royal family is a great honour.'

Something tweaked in the back of her brain. A memory from a news article she'd read a couple of weeks ago. His father had died. Recently.

Compassion moved through her, and empathy,

because she could vividly remember the pain of that loss. Five years ago, when her mother had died, she had felt as if she'd never be whole again. In time, day by day, she'd begun to feel more like herself, but it was still a work in progress. She felt her mother's absence every day.

It was that understanding that had her saying something she would normally not have dared. 'I'm sorry, about your father. Losing a parent is…we know it's something we should expect, but I don't think anything really prepares us for what life without them will be like.'

His eyes jolted to hers, widening in his face, so she immediately regretted her familiarity. He was a king, for goodness' sake, and her job was to bring the tea!

Dipping her head forward, she found she couldn't meet his eyes. 'If that's all, sir, goodnight.' She didn't wait for his answer; turning away from him, she strode to the concealed door. Her hand was on it when he spoke.

'Wait.'

She paused, her heart slamming against her ribcage.

She didn't turn around, though.

'Come back here.'

Her pulse was like a torrent in her veins.

She turned to face him. He was watching her.

Her heart rate accelerated to the point of, surely, danger.

'Yes, sir?'

A frown etched itself across his face. 'Sit.' He gestured to the sofas. 'Drink tea with me.'

A million reasons to say 'no' came to her. Not once in all the time she'd held this job had she come close to socialising with a guest. For one thing, it was completely forbidden in her contract.

*This is a professional establishment. They are not our friends. They are guests at the most exclusive hotel in the world.*

But that wasn't the only reason she was resisting his invitation.

He was too much. Too charming, too handsome, too completely masculine, and if her first, epic failure of a marriage had taught her anything, it was that men who were too handsome for their own good were not to be trusted.

'I insist.' His words cut through her hesitations, because, ultimately, he was asking her to join him for tea and surely that was within her job description? What the guests wanted, the guests got—within reason.

'I don't see how that will help you sleep,' she reminded him, gently.

His expression was like a whip cracking. 'Are you refusing?'

Panic had her shaking her head.

*Keep the guest happy, at all costs.*

'Of course not, sir.' She was already walking through the room, towards the sofas. Only one cup had been on the tray—besides, she didn't feel like persimmon tea. But she took a seat near the tray, her hands clasped neatly in her lap. And she waited for him to speak, her nerves stretching tighter and tighter with every silent beat that passed.

'Good.' His nod showed approval but it was hardly relaxing. The differences in their situations were apparent in every way. He was a king, his country renowned for its natural source of both oil and diamonds, making it hugely prosperous, with a chequered history of power-play as foreign forces sought to control both these natural resources for their own financial gain. Perhaps that explained the natural sense of power that exuded from every pore of his; he was a man born to rule a country that required a strong leader.

'Would you like a tea?'

'I think it would be rude to refuse,' she said quietly, but he heard, if the quirk of his brow was anything to go by.

'I have no interest in force-feeding you drinks native to my country. Would you prefer something else? Room service?'

The idea of anyone else seeing her sitting on the sofa talking to the Sheikh was impossible to contemplate.

'I'm fine.'

'You're sitting there as though you're half afraid I'm going to bite you.'

A small smile lifted Daisy's mouth. 'How should I be sitting, sir?'

He took the seat opposite, his own body language relaxed. His legs, long and muscled, were spread wide, and he lifted one arm along the back of the sofa. He looked so completely at home here, in this world of extreme luxury. That was hardly surprising, given he'd undoubtedly been raised in this kind of environment.

'However you would usually sit,' he prompted.

'I'm sorry,' she said, the words quizzical rather than apologetic. 'It's just this has never happened before.'

'No?'

'My job is to provide for your every need without actually being noticed.'

At that, his eyes flared wider, speculation colouring his irises for a heart-racing moment. 'I'm reasonably certain it would be impossible for you to escape anyone's notice.'

Heat rose in her cheeks, colouring them a pale pink that perfectly offset the golden tan of her complexion. She wasn't sure what to say to that, so she stayed quiet.

'Have you worked here long?'

She compressed her lips then stopped when his eyes followed the gesture, tracing the outline of her mouth in a way that made her tummy flip and flop.

'A few years.' She didn't add how hard that had been for her—to finally accept that her long-held dream of attending the Juilliard was beyond reach, once and for all.

'And always in this capacity?'

'I started in general concierge.' She crossed her legs, relaxing back into the seat a little. 'But about six months later, I was promoted to this position.'

'And you enjoy it?'

Of their own accord, her eyes drifted to the view of New York and her fingers tapped her knee, as if playing across the keys of the beloved piano she'd been forced to sell. 'I'm good at it.' She didn't catch the way his features shifted, respect moving over his face.

'How old are you?'

She turned back to face him, wondering how long he intended to keep her sitting there, knowing that it was very much within her job description to humour him even when this felt like an utterly bizarre way to spend her time.

'Twenty-four.'

'And you've always lived in America?'

'Yes.' She bit down on her lower lip thoughtfully. 'I've actually never even been overseas.'

His brows lifted. 'That's unusual, isn't it?'

She laughed softly. 'I don't know. You tell me?'

'It is.'

'Then I guess I'm unusual. Guilty as charged.'

'You don't have any interest in travelling?'

'Not having done something doesn't necessarily equate to a lack of interest,' she pointed out.

'So it's a lack of opportunity, then?'

He was rapier sharp, quickly able to read between the lines of anything she said.

'Yes.' Because there was no point in denying it.

'You work too much?'

'I work a lot,' she confirmed, without elaborating. There was no need to tell this man that she had more debt to her name than she'd likely ever be able to clear. Briefly, anger simmered in her veins, the kind of anger she only ever felt when she thought about one person: her waste-of-space ex-husband Max and the trouble he'd got her into.

'I thought you were guaranteed vacation time in the United States?'

Her smile was carefully constructed to dissuade further questioning along these lines, but, for good measure, she turned the tables on him. 'And you, sir? You travel frequently, I presume?'

His eyes narrowed as he studied her, and she had the strangest feeling he was pulling her apart, little by little, until he could see all the pieces that made her whole.

She held her breath, wondering if he was going to let the matter drop, and was relieved when he did.

'I do. Though never for long, and not lately.' His own features showed a tightness that she instinctively understood spoke of a desire not to be pressed on that matter.

But despite that, she heard herself say gently, 'Your father was ill for a while, before he died?'

The man's face paled briefly. He stood up, walking towards the window, his back rigid, his body tense. Daisy swallowed a curse. What was she thinking, asking something so personal? His father had just died—not even a month ago. She had no business inviting him to open that wound—and for a virtual stranger.

'I'm so sorry.' She stood, following him, bitterly regretting her big mouth. 'I had no right to ask you that. I'm sorry.' When he didn't speak, she swallowed, and said quietly, 'I'll leave you in peace now, Your Highness.'

# CHAPTER TWO

MANHATTAN WAS A vibrant hive of activity beyond the windows of his limousine. He kept his head back against the leather cushioning of his seat, his eyes focussed on nothing in particular.

'That could not have gone better, Your Highness.'

Malik was right. The speech to the United Nations had been a success. As he was talking, he realised that he wasn't the only one in the room who'd experienced anxiety about the importance of this. There was an air of tension, a fear that perhaps with the death of the great Kadir Al Antarah, they were to be plunged back into the days of war and violence that had marked too much of his country's history.

But Sariq was progressive, and Sariq was persuasive. He spoke of Shajarah, the capital of RKH, that had been born from the sands of the desert, its ancient soul nestled amongst the steel and glass monoliths that spoke of a place of the future, a place of promise. He spoke of his country's educational institutions which were free and world-class, of his belief that education was the best prevention for war and violence, that a literate and informed people were less likely to care for ancient wounds. He highlighted what the people of RKH had in common with the rest of the world and when he was finished, there was widespread applause.

Yes, the speech had been a success, but still there was a kernel of discontent within his gut. A feeling of dissatisfaction he couldn't explain.

'Your father would have been proud of you, sir.'

Malik was right about that too.

'When we return to the hotel, have the concierge come to me,' Sariq told Malik. He didn't know her name. That was an oversight he would remedy.

'Is there something you require?'

'She will see to it.'

If Malik thought the request strange, he didn't say anything. The limousine cut east across Manhattan, snagging in traffic near Bryant Park, so Sariq stared from his window at the happy scene there. The day had been warm and New Yorkers had taken to the park to feel the brief respite from the temperature offered by the lush surrounds. He watched as a child reached into the fountain and scooped some water out, splashing it at his older brother, and his chest panged with a sense of acceptance.

Children were as much a part of his future as ruling was. He was the last heir of the Al Antarah line of Kings, a line that had begun at the turn of the last millennia. When he returned to his kingdom and his people, he would focus more seriously on that. He knew the risks if he didn't, the likelihood of civil war that would result from a dangerous fight for the throne of the country.

Marriage, children, these things would absolve him of that worry and would secure his country's future for generations to come.

'You wanted to see me, Your Highness?' Her heart was in her throat. She'd barely slept since she'd left his apartment the night before, despite the fact she'd been rostered off during the day, while he was engaged on official business. That was how it worked when she had high-profile guests. She knew their schedules intimately so she could form her day around their movements, thus ensuring her availability when they were likely to need her.

He was not alone, and he was not as he'd been the night before—dressed simply in jeans and a shirt. Now, he wore a white robe, flowing and long, with gold embellishments on the sleeve, and on his head there was a traditional *keffiyeh* headdress, white and fastened in place with a gold cord. It was daunting and powerful and she found her mouth was completely dry as she regarded him with what she hoped was an impassive expression. That was hard to manage when her knees seemed to have a desire to knock together.

'Yes. One moment.'

His advisors wore similar outfits, though less embellished. It was clear that his had a distinction of royal rank. She stood where she was as they continued speaking in their own language, the words beautiful and musical, the Sheikh's voice discernible amongst all others. It was ten minutes before they began to disband, moving away from the Sheikh, each with a low bow of respect, which he acknowledged with a small nod sometimes, and other times not at all.

His fingers were long and tanned, and on one finger he wore a gold ring with a small, rounded face, like a Super Bowl ring, she thought out of nowhere and smiled at the idea of this man on the football field. He'd probably take to it like a duck to water, if his physique was anything to go by. Beneath those robes, she knew he had the build of a natural athlete.

Great.

Her mouth was dry all over again but this

time he was sweeping towards her, his robes flowing behind him. She had only a few seconds to attempt to calm her racing pulse.

When he was a few feet away from her, he paused, so she was caught up in the masculinity of his fragrance, the exotic addictiveness of it—citrus and pine needles, spice and sunshine.

'You were offended last night.'

His words were the last thing she'd expected. Heat bloomed in her cheeks.

'I was too familiar, sir.' She dropped her eyes to the view, unable to look at him, a thousand and one butterflies rampaging wildly inside her belly.

'I invited you to be familiar,' he reminded her so the butterflies gave way to a roller coaster.

'Still…' she lifted her shoulders, risking a glance at him then wishing she hadn't when she discovered his eyes were piercing her own '… I shouldn't have…'

'He had been sick. It was unpleasant to witness. I wished, more than anything, that I could do something to alleviate his pain.' A muscle jerked in his jaw and his eyes didn't shift from hers. 'I have been raised to believe in the full extent of my power, and yet I was impotent against the ravages of his disease. No doctor anywhere could save him, nor really help him.' He didn't move and yet somehow she felt closer to him, as though she'd swayed forward without realising it.

'Your question last night is difficult for me to answer.'

'I'm sorry.'

'Don't be. You didn't do anything wrong.'

Her body was in overdrive, every single sense pulling through her, and she was aware, in the small part of her brain that was capable of rational thought, that this was a completely foreign territory to be in. He was a guest of the hotel—their boundaries were clearly established.

She had to find a way to get them back onto more familiar territory.

'I work for the hotel,' she said quietly. 'Asking you personal questions isn't within my job description, and it's certainly not appropriate. It won't happen again.'

He didn't react to that. He stayed exactly where he was, completely still, like a sentinel, watching her, his eyes trained on her face in a way that made her pulse stutter.

'I asked you to talk with me,' he reminded her finally.

'But I should have declined.'

'Your job is to facilitate my needs, is it not?'

Her heart began to pound against her ribs. 'Within reason.'

His smile showed a hint of something she

couldn't interpret. ~~Cynicism? Mockery?~~ Frustration?

'Are you saying that if I ask you to come and sit with me again tonight, you'll refuse?'

Her body was filled with lava, so hot she could barely breathe.

Her eyes were awash with uncertainty. 'I'm not sure it's appropriate.'

'What are you afraid of?'

'Honestly?'

He was watchful.

'I'm afraid of saying the wrong thing. Of offending you. My job is to silently…'

'Yes, yes, you have told me this. To escape notice. And I told you that's not possible. I have already noticed you, Daisy. And having had the pleasure of speaking with you once, I would like to repeat that—with a less abrupt conclusion this time. Are you saying therefore that you won't sit with me?'

Her chest felt as though it had been cracked open. 'Um, yes, I am, I think.' She dropped her eyes to the shining floor.

Because I enjoyed talking to you, too, she amended inwardly, fully aware that she was moving into a territory that was lined with danger.

'But if you're worried you offended me, let me assure you, I am not easily offended,' he offered, and now he smiled, in a way that was like forcing sunshine into a darkened room. Her breath burned in her lungs.

'Frankly, I'd be surprised if you were.'

'Then you can bring me tea tonight. I have a dinner but Malik will send for you when it's done.'

He had no idea what he was doing. The American woman was beautiful, but it had been a long time since Sariq had considered beauty to be a requirement in a woman he was interested in. Besides, he couldn't be seriously interested in her. His duty was clear: to return to the RKH and marry, so that he could begin the process of shoring up his lineage. There were two women whom it would make sense to marry and he would need to choose one, and promptly.

Enjoying the companionship of his hotel's concierge seemed pointless and futile, and yet he found himself turning his attention to his watch every few minutes throughout the state dinner, willing it to be over so he could call for a tray of tea and the woman with eyes the colour of the sky on a winter's morning.

She had asked the kitchen to prepare tea for two, with no further explanation. And even though they had no way of knowing the Sheikh wasn't entertaining in his suite, she felt a flush of guilt as she took the tray, as though surely everyone must know that she was about to cross an invisible line in the sand and socialise with a guest.

Calm down, she insisted to herself as the elevator sped towards the top of the building. It's just tea and conversation, hardly a hanging offence. He was grieving and despite the fact he was surrounded by an entourage, she could easily imagine how lonely his position must be, how refreshing to meet someone who hadn't been indoctrinated into the ways of worshipping at his feet by virtue of the fact that he ruled the land from which they heralded.

This was no different from the other unusual requests she had been asked to fulfil, it was just a lot harder to delegate. He wanted *her*. To talk to her. She couldn't say why—she wasn't particularly interesting, which filled her with anxiety at the job before her, but, for whatever reason, he had been insistent.

She knocked at the door then pushed it inwards. He was standing almost exactly where he'd been the night before, still wearing the robes he had been in earlier that day, though he'd removed the headpiece, so her heart rate trebled. Because he looked so impossibly handsome, so striking with his tanned skin and strong body encased in the crisp white and gold.

It brought out a hint of blond in his hair that she hadn't noticed at first, just a little at the ends, which spoke of a tendency to spend time outdoors.

He walked towards her so she stood completely still, as though her legs were planted to the floor, and when his hands curved around the edges of the tray, it was impossible for them not to brush hers. A jolt of electricity burst through her, splitting her into a thousand pieces so she had to work hard not to visibly react.

'I'm pleased you came.'

He stood there, watching her, for a beat too long and then took the tray, placing it on the coffee table.

'The first reference to persimmon tea comes from one of our earliest texts. In the year forty-seven AD, a Bedouin tribe brought it as a gift to the people of the west of my country. Their skill with harvesting the fruit late in the season and drying them in such a way as to preserve the flavour made them popular with traders.'

He poured some into a cup and held it in front of him, waiting, a small smile on his lips that did funny things to her tummy.

She forced her legs to carry her across the room, a tight smile of her own crossing her expression as she took the teacup. 'Thank you.'

He was watching her and so she took a small sip, her eyes widening at the flavour. 'It's so sweet. Like honey.'

He made a throaty noise of agreement. 'Picked at the right time, persimmons are sweet. Dried slowly, that intensifies, until you get this.'

She took another sip, her insides warming to the flavour. It was like drinking happiness. Why had she resisted so long?

'Are you going to have some?'

'I don't feel like sleeping tonight.'

Her stomach lurched and she chattered the cup against the saucer a little too loudly, shooting him a look that was half apology, half warning.

She had to keep this professional. It was imperative that she not forget who she was, who he was, and why her job mattered so much to her. She was lucky with this position. She earned a salary that was above and beyond what she could have hoped, by virtue of her untarnished ability to provide exemplary customer service. One wrong move and her reputation would suffer, so too would her job, potentially, and she couldn't jeopardise that.

It helped to imagine her manager in the room, observing their conversation. If she pictured Henry watching, she could keep things professional and light, she could avoid the gravitational pull that seemed to be dragging on her.

'You were at the United Nations today, sir?'

A quirk shifted his lips, but he nodded. 'It was my first official speech as ruler of the RKH.'

'How did it go?'

He gestured towards the sofa, inviting her to sit. She chose one side, crossing her legs primly and placing the cup and saucer on her knee, holding it with both hands.

He took the seat beside her, not opposite, so she was aware of his every movement, the shift of his body dragging on the cushions on the sofa, inadvertently pulling her towards him.

'I was pleased with the reception.'

She sipped her tea, forcing herself to relax. 'I can't imagine having to do that,' she confided with a small smile. After all, he wanted to talk to her—sitting there like a petrified automaton wasn't particularly conversational. 'I'm terrible at public speaking. I hate it. I feel everyone's eyes burning me and just want to curl up in a ball for ever.'

'It's a skill you can learn.'

'Perhaps. But fortunately for me, I don't need to.'

Silence prickled at their sides.

She spoke to fill it. 'I don't feel like you would have needed to do much learning there.'

He frowned. 'I don't understand.'

'Sorry, that wasn't clear.' She shook her head. 'I just mean you were probably born with this innate ability to stand in front of a group of people and enthral them.'

She clamped her mouth shut, wishing she

hadn't come so close to admitting that she was a little bit enthralled by him.

He smiled though, in a way that relaxed her and warmed her. 'I was born knowing my destiny. I was born to be Sheikh, ruler of my people, and, as such, never imagined what it would be like to…avoid notice.' His eyes ran over her face speculatively, so even as she was relaxing, she was also vibrating in a way that was energising and demanding.

'I don't think you'd be very good at it.'

'At being Sheikh?'

'At avoiding notice.'

'Nor are you, so this we have in common.'

Heat spread through her veins like wildfire.

'I don't think you see me clearly,' she said after a moment.

'No?'

'I'm very good at not being seen.'

His laugh was husky. 'It's quite charming that you think so.'

She shook her head a little. 'I don't really understand…'

'You are a beautiful young woman with hair the colour of desert sand and eyes like the sky. Even in this boxy uniform, you are very, very noticeable.'

She stared at him for several seconds, pleasure at war with uncertainty. Remember Max, she reminded herself. He'd noticed her. He'd praised her, flattered her, and she'd fallen for it so fast she hadn't stopped to heed any of the warning signs. And look how that had turned out!

'Thank you.' It was stiff, an admonishment.

He laughed. 'You are not good with compliments.'

She bit down on her lip, their situation troubling her, pulling on her. 'I should go.'

He reached a hand out, pressing it to her knee. Her skin glowed where he'd touched her, filling her with a scattering sensation of pins and needles. 'No more compliments,' he promised. 'Tell me about yourself, Daisy Carrington.'

Her eyes flared wide. 'How do you know my surname?'

'I asked my chief of security.'

'How…?'

'All hotel staff are independently vetted by my agencies,' he explained, as though that were no big deal.

Her lips parted. 'Then I suspect you know more about me than I realised.'

'It's not comprehensive,' he clarified. 'Your name, date of birth, any links to criminal activity.' He winked. 'You were clear, by the way.'

Despite herself, she smiled. 'I'm pleased to hear it.'

'May I call you Daisy?'

'So long as you don't expect me to call you anything other than Your Highness,' she quipped.

'Very well. So, Daisy? Before you started working here, what did you do?'

Her stomach clenched. Remembered pain was there, pushing against her. She thought of her marriage, her divorce, her acceptance to the Juilliard, and pushed them all away. 'This and that.' A tight smile, showing more than she realised.

'Which tells me precisely nothing.'

'I worked in hospitality.'

'And it's what you have always wanted to do?'

The question hurt. She didn't talk about her music. It was too full of pain—pain remembering her father, and the way he'd sat beside her, moving her fingers over the keys until they learned the path themselves, the way she'd stopped playing the day he'd left. And then, when her mother was in her low patches, the way Daisy had begun to play again—it was the only thing she had responded to.

'It's what I gravitated to.'

'Another answer that tells me nothing.'

Because she was trying to obfuscate but he was too clever for that. What was the harm in being honest with him? He had reserved this suite for four nights—this was his second. He would be gone soon and she'd never see him again.

'I wanted to be a concert pianist, actually.'

He went very still, his eyes hooked to hers, waiting, watching. And she found the words spilling out of her even when she generally made a habit of not speaking them. After all, what good could come from reliving a fantasy lost?

'My father was a jazz musician. He taught me to play almost from infancy. I would sit beside him and he would arrange my fingers, and when we weren't playing, we would listen to music, so I was filled with its unique language, all the beats that mixed together to make a song, to tell a story and weave a narrative with their melody. I love all types of music, but classical is my favourite. I lose myself in Chopin and Mozart, so that I'm barely conscious of the passage of time.'

He stared at her, his surprise evident, and with little wonder. It was as though the words had burst from her, so full of passion and memory, so alive with her love and regrets.

'Do you play?'

A beat passed, a silence, as he contemplated this. 'No. My mother did, and very well.' Another pause, and, though his expression didn't shift, she had a feeling he was choosing his words with care. 'After she died, my father had all the pianos removed from the palace. He couldn't bear to hear them played. Music was not a big part of my upbringing.'

Her heart twisted in her chest. The pain of losing a mother was one she was familiar with. 'How old were you?'

A tight smile. 'Seven.'

The tightness in her chest increased. 'I'm sorry.'

He nodded. 'As am I. Her death was a grief from which my father never recovered.'

'The flipside to a great love.'

'Speaking from experience?'

Her denial was swift and visceral. 'No.'

Though she'd been married, she could see now that she'd never loved Max. She'd felt grateful to him, glad to have someone in her life after her mother's death.

'My mom died five years ago, and not a day passes when I don't think of her in some small way. At this time of year, when the sunflowers in the street are all in bloom, I ache to take photos for her. She loved that, you know. *Only in New York would you get sunflowers as street plantings.*' Her smile was wistful.

'How did she…?'

Daisy's throat thickened unexpectedly. 'A car accident.' She didn't elaborate—that her mother had been responsible. That she'd driven into a lamppost after drinking half a bottle of gin.

They sat in silence for several moments, but it was no longer a prickly, uncomfortable silence. On the contrary, Daisy felt an odd sense of peace wrap around her, a comfortable fog that made her want to stay exactly where she was.

It was the warning she needed, and she jolted herself out of her silent reflection, forcing herself to stand.

'I really should go, sir. It's late and I'm sure you have more important things to do than talk to me.'

As with the night before, he didn't try to stop her. She ignored the kernel of disappointment and stalked to the door, pulling it inwards. But before leaving him, she turned back to regard him over her shoulder.

'Goodnight, Your Highness. Sleep well.'

# CHAPTER THREE

'HE'S ASKING FOR YOU.'

Daisy had just walked in through the door of the hotel, and she shot a glance at her watch. It was after ten o'clock at night. The Sheikh was supposed to be at a party until midnight. She'd come in early to settle her nerves, and to mentally prepare her excuses in case he called for her to come and talk to him again.

Henry grimaced apologetically. 'He seems more demanding than most.'

'No, he's not really.'

'You sure? You could get Amy to take care of him. She's already been up there a few times today.'

Daisy thought of the woman who'd been recruited to shadow Daisy, taking care of Daisy's clients when Daisy couldn't. Instinctively, she pushed the idea aside.

'He's a very important guest, Henry. It should be me. You should have called.'

'I don't want you getting burned out, love. You can't work around the clock. We can't afford to lose you.'

'I'm fine.' Her heart twisted in her chest. She'd been buzzing with a heady sense of anticipation all day, waiting to see him, wondering if he'd call for her, or if wisdom and sense would have prevailed so that he woke up and wondered why the heck he was bothering to spend so much time talking to a servant.

'When did he call?'

'An hour ago.'

Panic lurched through her. 'Why didn't you page me?'

'He said to tell you to go up when you arrived. I knew you wouldn't be long...'

'Henry,' she wailed, shaking her head. 'What if it was something urgent?'

'Then that Malik man would have made himself known.' Henry exaggerated a shudder. 'He has no problems demanding whatever the hell he wants, when he wants it.'

That was true. Up until recently, all the requests had come from Malik. 'I'll go up now.'

She reached for the buzzer, to order some persimmon tea, but the kitchen informed her the Presidential suite had already requested dinner. 'It should only be another few minutes.'

'I thought he was at a function.'

'Dunno,' came the unhelpful response, so Daisy frowned as she disconnected the call. Double-checking her appearance in the mirror, she wished her cheeks weren't so pink, nor her eyes so shining with obvious pleasure. The truth was, she couldn't wait to see him, and that was dangerous.

Because he was going home soon, and, even if he weren't, he was just a client. A client who was developing a habit of asking for her in the evenings.

She took the service elevator to the top floor, so the doors whooshed inwards and she knocked once. Before she could step inside, the door was pulled inwards and Sariq stood on the other side. He was wearing more familiar clothes this time—a pair of dark jeans and a white tee shirt with a vee at the neck that revealed a hint of curls at his throat.

Damn it, out of nowhere she found herself wondering how far down his hair went, imagining him without his shirt, and that made it almost impossible to keep a veneer of professionalism on her face.

'Thank you for coming.'

'It's my job,' she reminded him.

He didn't move, but his eyes glowed with something that could have been amusement and could have been cynicism. If it was the latter, she didn't have to wonder at why: it was pretty obvious that her being there had very little to do with her professional obligations.

'I thought you had something on tonight.'

'It didn't last as long as the schedule had allowed,' he said simply, drawing the door open without stepping far enough aside, so in order to enter the suite, she had to brush past him, and the second their bodies connected she felt a rush of awareness that was impossible to ignore. Instinctively, her face lifted to his and she saw the raw speculation there; the same interest that flooded her veins was rushing through his. Her knees shuddered and heat pooled between her legs, making thought, speech and movement almost impossible.

He stood so close, their bodies were touching. Just lightly, but enough, and even when Daisy knew she should move, or say something, she couldn't. She could only stare at him. His face was like thunder, but his eyes were all flame. She could feel the war being raged within him, a battle to control his desire, and she didn't want him to. This was madness. It was sheer, uncontrollable madness—and she had a billion reasons to resist. Max was the main one—her experience with him had warned her off tempestuous affairs for life. But she'd married Max, she'd pledged to love him and trust him, to spend the rest of her life with him. That had been her mistake. The Sheikh was only in New York for two more nights, including this one.

But he was a guest in the hotel! A seriously important guest, and she couldn't afford to have anything go wrong. She swallowed, taking a step backwards, except she forgot there was a piece of furniture there and her hip jabbed into it, shunting her sideways, so she might have fallen if he hadn't pushed a hand out, confidently, easily righting her. Her eyes were alarmed as they lifted to his and stuck there like glue, and when he took a step towards her, she couldn't look away.

Her heart was hammering against her ribs so hard and fast that she was surprised he couldn't see its frantic movements against her breasts. If she pushed up onto the tips of her toes, if she lifted her face, oh, God, she wanted to kiss him. The realisation was like fire, even when she knew it should have doused her desire, that it should have dragged her back to reality and put a halt to this foolishness.

But was it so foolish? Daisy had played it safe for so long and, suddenly, she was sick of it. Sick of playing it safe, of being careful with whom she trusted. It was as though she second-guessed her instincts so often that they'd grown blunt.

'Your Highness…' She wasn't sure what she wanted to say, only that they were standing so close, staring at one another, sensual heat heavy in the air around them, and she wanted to act on it. She wanted him.

But he frowned, his eyes darkening, even as he dropped his head closer. 'I asked you here to show you something.'

Neither of them moved.

'What is it?'

He lifted a hand, as though he couldn't resist, pressing his thumb and forefinger to her chin so he could hold her face where it was, lifted towards him. The contact was so personal, it felt as though they'd crossed a line they couldn't uncross. They could no longer pretend this wasn't happening. They were acknowledging the pull that ran between them.

'I wasn't going to do this.'

'Do what?'

With his body in the door frame, he dropped his head by a matter of degrees, so there was ample time for her to move, to say something, to stop this. She didn't. She stayed where she was, her face held in his fingers, her body swaying a little closer to his so her breasts brushed his chest and, through the fine fabric of his shirt and her blouse, she was sure he must feel the hardening of her nipples, the way they strained against her lace bra.

'I swore I wouldn't.' And then, his mouth claimed hers, his kiss fierce, filled with all the passion of having fought this, of having felt desire and resisted it for as long as he was able.

It was a kiss born of need and it surged inside her, his lips pushing hers apart, his tongue driving into her mouth, his other hand lifting and pushing into her hair, his fingers cradling her head, holding her against him so he could plunder her mouth, tasting her, his body so big and broad compared to hers that she felt utterly enveloped by him, swallowed by his strength and power, her senses subsumed completely by this.

It was a kiss of oblivion, so consuming that she didn't hear the dinging of the lift doors. She was lost completely in this moment but he wasn't. He broke the kiss swiftly, his body in the door frame concealing her. 'Go to my room.' His eyes held a warning that she heeded even when nothing made sense and her body could scarcely move. She'd been in the suite enough times to know where the master bedroom was. She ran there, pushing the door shut except for an inch, so she could peer out.

She saw members of the kitchen team walk into the apartment, each pausing to bow for the Sheikh, before moving to the table and setting it. Sariq's eyes chased hers, down the corridor, so she moved away from the door, pressing her back against a wall and closing her eyes, needing her heart to slow down, her breathing to return to normal. She lifted her fingers to her lips; they were sensitive to the touch.

She was grateful beyond belief for his quick thinking. If it had been up to her, she would have stayed where she was, and someone from the staff would have seen her and rumours would have been flying. His quick response had saved her from that embarrassment. What would Henry say? Mortified, she fanned her face and tucked her shirt in more tightly—it had become loose at her waist, and she paced the room as she waited. It didn't take long. A few minutes and then she heard the click of a door, the turning of a lock, and they were alone once more.

She pulled the door to his bedroom open, moving into the lounge area to find him uncorking a bottle of wine and pouring two glasses. His eyes, when they met hers, were loaded with speculation.

'I ordered us dinner.'

Her eyes moved to the table. Surprise usurped whatever she'd been feeling a moment ago. 'You did? Why?'

His smile was without humour. 'Because we have to eat.'

She sighed heavily. 'I don't have to eat with you, though, Your Highness.'

'I can taste your kiss in my mouth,' he murmured. 'Don't you think it's time you called me something else?'

His words were so evocative but she shook her head. 'You're my client. That should never have happened...'

He paced across the room, handing her the wine glass. She took it without taking a drink. He stayed close to her, his body's contact intimate and loaded with promise. 'It shouldn't,' he agreed, after a moment. 'But it did, and I think we both know it will happen again. And again. So let's stop pretending we don't want this.'

Her eyes flared wide. Need punctured sense almost completely—but not quite. 'I can't afford to lose my job.'

She felt his naked speculation. 'Do you think I'm going to jeopardise that?'

'Socialising with clients is strictly forbidden. It's actually in my contract. And what we just did goes way beyond socialising.'

'I have my own reasons for requiring discretion,' he said firmly. 'Whatever happens between us, no one will know.'

*Whatever happens between us.* The words glowed with promise. Her insides quivered.

'Nothing can happen.'

'Why not?'

'I told you, my job…' but she wasn't even convincing herself.

'And I told you, no one will find out. Do you have a boyfriend?'

'No.' How long had it been since she'd been with a man? That was easy. Max. He was her only lover. He'd been her first, and when they'd divorced three years ago, she thought he'd be her last.

'I think you want me.' His words held a challenge. He took her wine glass from her, sipping from it and then placing it on the table to his left. His eyes glowed with the same challenge as he lifted his fingers to the top button of her blouse.

'I am going to undo these buttons very slowly, giving you plenty of time to ask me to stop. If you say the word, then it's over. You can go away again.' He did as he'd promised, his fingers working deftly to undo the first button, so she felt a brush of air against her skin. Then the next, exposing the top of her lace bra. The next revealed the midsection of the bra and, with the next button, the shirt gaped enough to reveal it completely. At the last button, his fingers slowed.

'You haven't asked me to stop.'

Her eyes were awash with feelings. 'I know that.'

'I want to make love to you.'

'I know that too.'

He turned towards the table. 'Are you hungry?'

She shook her head.

'You don't want anything to eat?'

Another shift of her head to indicate 'no'.

'What do you want, Daisy?'

The final button was separated, so her shirt fell apart completely.

She opened her mouth, but found it hard to frame any words.

'Do you want to know what I want?' he murmured, dropping his head to whisper the words against the sensitive flesh at the base of her throat.

'I think I can guess.' And despite the heavy pulsing of emotion that was filling the room, she smiled, because it was easy to smile in that moment.

He smiled back, but it was dredged from deep within him, so it cut across his face, his lips like a blade.

His grief was palpable. It had been since the first moment they'd met and it was there now, tormenting him, so that this physical act of sensuality took on a new imperative. She understood the power sex held, the power to obliterate grief and pain, even if only for a moment.

Wasn't it her own grief that had made her so vulnerable to Max? He'd promised respite from her sadness and she'd ignored all the warning signs to grab that respite. Was Sariq doing the same thing now?

Should she be putting a halt to this to save him from regret?

His fingers were on the straps of her bra, easing them down her arms so tiny goose bumps danced where his fingertips touched, and his eyes were on her breasts as he pushed aside the scrap of lace, so she felt a burning heat in her chest and a tingling in her nipples, an ache that begged him to touch her, to feel the weight of her breasts in his palms, to touch her nipples, to kiss them.

Her back swayed forward, the invitation silent but imperative, and he understood, lifting his hands to her hips first, bracing her waist as he drew his touch upwards, along her sides until his thumbs swept beneath her breasts and she tipped her head back a little on a plea, biting down on her lip to stop what she knew would be incoherent babbling, the kind of babbling brought on by a form of madness.

'I need you to tell me you want this.' He drew his kiss from her lips to her throat, flicking the pulse point there, dragging his stubbled jaw across her sensitive flesh. She pushed her body forward, her hips moving from side to side, her hands pushing his shirt up so her fingertips could run over his chest. God, his chiselled, firm chest. Her nails drew along the ridges of each muscular bump, running higher so her hands curved over his shoulders, feeling the warmth of his flesh and the beating of his heart against her forearm.

'Daisy?' It was a groan and a plea. His body was tense. He was waiting for her to say that she wanted this and something inside her trembled, because it was such a mark of respect and decency. It wasn't that she hadn't expected it from Sariq, it was that she hadn't known to expect it from anybody. Max had been… She didn't want to think about Max in that moment. He'd already taken so much from her, she wasn't going to give him this moment too. It was hers, hers and Sariq's.

'I want this.' The words blurted out of her. And then, more gently, but the same bone-melting urgency. 'I want *you*.' She couldn't resist adding, with an impish smile: 'Your Highness.'

He lifted a brow, his lips quirking in a smile that was impulsive and so sexy. But he swallowed and the smile disappeared, his expression serious once more. 'I have to go back to the RKH as scheduled. I cannot offer more than this.'

Another sign of respect. Her heart felt all warm and gooey and her voice was husky. 'I know that.' She showed her acceptance by pushing up and kissing him, by wrapping her arms around his waist, holding him close to her body so she could feel the force of his urgent need through their clothing. 'Take me to bed, sir.'

*'Take me to bed, sir.'*

He didn't need to be asked again. He lifted her up, cradling her against his chest as he carried her through the suite and into the master bedroom. He didn't pause to turn on a light, though he would love to have revelled in her beauty, staring at her as he pleasured her: there'd be time for that. Having abandoned himself to this, he intended to enjoy her all night. He knew this would be the last time he acted on impulses such as this, the last time he allowed himself to be simply a man and not a king. Soon he would announce his engagement and he would be faithful to the bride of his choosing.

Until then though, there was this, and he was going to enjoy it. He disposed of her clothes quickly, no longer able to pace himself; he needed to feel every inch of her beneath him. Her legs were smooth and slender. He ran his palms over her flesh as he stripped her of the uniform she wore, acknowledging to himself he'd wanted to do exactly that from the first moment he'd seen her. His own clothes followed next so he stood above her naked. The room was dark but he could make out her silhouette against the bed, her blonde hair shimmering gold in the darkness. He brought the full weight of his body down on hers, his arousal pressing between her legs so, for the briefest moment, he fantasised about taking her like that. No protection, no preamble, just white-hot possession.

She arched her back and lifted her legs around his waist, drawing him towards her, as though she wanted that too. He kissed her, hard, his tongue doing to her mouth what his body wished it could do in that moment, and she met his kiss with every stroke, pushing her body up onto her elbows, wanting more of him, needing him in the way he needed her. Her feet at his back were insistent, pushing him towards her, so he let just his tip press to her sex, her hot, wet body welcoming him in a way he knew he had to control. He swore in his own language, pulling away from her with effort, his breathing ragged.

'Wait.' He stood up and her cry was an animalistic sound of disbelief, her need reaching out and wrapping around him. 'One moment,' he reassured her, moving to the adjoining bathroom and pulling a condom out of a travel bag. He didn't make a habit of this—he couldn't remember the last time he'd slept with a woman he'd just met—but he was always prepared, regardless.

Striding back into the room, he pushed the rubber over his length as he went, inviting no further delay to this. Her eyes were difficult to make out in this darkness but he thought he saw a hint of apology in the light thrown from the bathroom.

'I forgot,' she explained, reaching for him.

'I almost did too.'

'Thank you. For remembering.'

He kissed her more gently, reassuringly, parting her thighs with his palm and locking himself against her, as he had been before. She lifted her hips and this time, he didn't hold himself back. He drove his cock into her, his hands digging into her hips to hold her steady as he took control of her body and made her, completely, his.

# CHAPTER FOUR

IT WAS A pleasure unlike any she'd ever known. Her breathing was heavy as she lay on his bed, waiting for sanity, normality, reason to intrude. Her orgasm—no, her *orgasms*, because he'd driven her over the edge of pleasure several times in a row—was still dissipating, her body felt heavy and weak at the same time as strong beyond belief, and his body, spent at last, was heavy on hers, his own breathing torn from him with silent torment. She ran her fingernails down his back, his skin warm and smooth, curving over his buttocks, and she smiled like the cat that'd got the cream.

Professionally, this had the potential to be a complete disaster, but in that moment, she didn't care. She pushed up and kissed his shoulder, tasting salt there and moaning softly. He was still inside her and she felt him respond, his beautiful cock jerking at her kiss. A sense of power swelled inside her, because he was as much of a slave to this as she was.

'I…didn't think that would happen when I came here tonight,' she said, when finally her breathing had slowed sufficiently to enable her to speak.

He pushed up on one elbow, so she could make out the features of his face against the darkness of the room. 'Do you regret it?'

'Nope.'

His teeth were white, so she could see them in his smile. 'Me neither.' He dropped a kiss to one of her temples and then pushed away from her, standing and striding towards the bathroom. When he opened the door, more light flooded the room. She was so familiar with its décor but now she saw it through new eyes—and always would. He would leave soon, and someone else would occupy this suite of rooms, but the rooms would be overlaid with ghosts of her time with the Sheikh of the RKH for ever.

'I've never done this before,' she blurted out, hating the thought of him believing this was a regular occurrence for her. He reappeared, a towel wrapped around his waist, and now he reached for the wall and flicked a light on, so she was stark naked against the crisp white hotel sheets. She reached for the quilt, at the foot of the bed, pulling it up to cover herself.

'Don't.' And he was imperious, a ruler of a country, his command used to being obeyed. She stilled, her eyes lifting to his. 'I want to see you.'

Her mouth went dry, her throat completely thick, as he stood where he was but let his eyes feast upon her body. And she let him, remaining where she was, naked and exposed, her flesh marked with patches of red from where his stubbled jaw had grated against her, or where his mouth had kissed and sucked her flesh until it grew pink. Her cheeks were warm but still she stayed where she was, grateful there was no mirror within eye line that could show her the picture she made, or self-consciousness might have dictated that she ignore him and seek cover.

But she wouldn't have anyway, because the look in his face was so loaded with admiration and pleasure, with need and desire, that she could do nothing but lie there and watch him enjoy her. It was ridiculous, given how completely he'd satisfied her, but desire began to roll through her like an unrelenting wave, so she was full of want for him all over again.

It was so different from how she'd felt about Max. When they'd made love it had been…nice, at best. He hadn't ever driven her to orgasm, and he sure as heck hadn't seemed to care. But the closeness had been welcome, and she'd been too caught up in his lies by then to question whether it was enough for her.

'I didn't know it could be like this,' she whispered, unable to hold his eyes at the admission. She heard him approaching her, then felt his hands reaching for hers, pulling her to a sitting position first then to stand in front of him.

'No?' A gravelled question, his eyes roaming her face. She kept her gaze focussed to the right of his shoulder.

She didn't feel any need to obfuscate the truth with this man, even when the difference in their experience level might have rationally caused her to feel a little immature and embarrassed. 'My ex…my ex-husband…and I weren't exactly…we never…it wasn't like this.' She finished with a frustrated shake of her head. 'Now I get what all the fuss is about.'

He was very still, his Adam's apple jerking in his throat. 'You were married?'

'A long time ago.'

'You're twenty-four years old. It can't have been that long…'

'I left him a week after my twenty-first birthday.' Some present. Finding that her bank accounts had been emptied, and a mortgage taken out on her mother's home. All the security she'd thought she'd had, after her mother's death, had evaporated alongside the marriage she'd believed to be a decent one.

He lifted his hands, cupping her cheeks, and now when she looked at him he was staring at her in that magical way of his, as though he could read her mind when she wasn't speaking.

'Do you want to talk about it?'

'No.' She smiled to soften the blunt refusal. 'He took enough from me. I don't want to let him into this, with you.'

Curiosity flared in his gaze, and anger too, but not directed at her. It was the opposite. She felt his anger directed at Max and it was somehow bonding and reassuring—in that the whole 'enemy of my enemy is my friend' kind of way.

'He was a bastard,' she said, the small elaboration a courtesy, more than anything. 'I'm better off without him.'

His nod was short. 'The food will be cold. Are you hungry?'

'I have no objection to cold food,' she assured him quickly. 'Besides, I'd rather not be interrupted.'

He expelled a slow breath, a sound of relief. 'I'm glad you're not planning on running away again.'

She lifted a brow. 'I think you've given me incentive to stick around. At least for a little while.'

His laugh was husky. He weaved his fingers through hers and drew her towards the door of the bedroom but she stopped walking. 'My clothes.' He was, after all, wearing a towel around his hips.

He paused, turning to face her thoughtfully before dropping her hand and pacing to the pile of fabric on the floor. He liberated her silk underpants, crossing to her and crouching at her feet, holding them for her to step into. She pressed a hand to his shoulder to steady herself, and he eased the underwear up her legs. But at her thighs, he paused, bringing his head forward and pressing a kiss to the top, so she trembled against him and might have lost her balance were it not for the grip on his shoulder. She felt his smile against her flesh.

Another kiss, nearer her womanhood, and then his mouth was there, his tongue pressing against her sex until he found her most sensitive cluster of nerves and tormented it with his ministrations, tasting her, teasing her, sucking her until she exploded in a blinding explosion. She dug her nails into his skin and she cried into the room, pleasure making her incoherent.

He lifted his head, his eyes on hers, his expression impossible to discern, and then he lifted her underpants into place, standing as he did so.

'No more clothes.'

Her heart was racing too fast to permit her to speak.

'I like looking at you.'

The words were delivered with the power that she knew came instinctively to him, and even when there was a part of her that might have felt self-conscious, his obvious admiration drove that away, so she shrugged, incapable of speaking.

'Good.' His approval warmed her. 'Come and eat.'

She was surprisingly hungry, so the feast he'd ordered was a welcome surprise. She hadn't seen it being delivered and unpacked, but it looked as though he'd had a feast of foods prepared, their exotic fragrance making her mouth water.

'Delicacies from the RKH,' he explained. 'Fish with okra and spice.' He pointed to one dish. 'Lamb with olives and couscous, chicken and pomegranate, spinach and raisin flat bread, and aubergine and citrus tagine.'

'Wow.' She stared at the banquet. 'This was just for you?'

'I suspected you'd join me.'

She laughed softly. 'Am I that predictable?'

'I'm that determined,' he corrected softly, running a finger over her arm so she trembled with sensations. 'I wanted you from the moment I saw you.'

'And you always get what you want?'

Darkness coloured his expression for a moment and she could have kicked herself. He was grieving his father's premature death—obviously that wasn't the case.

'Not always, no.'

She nodded, glad he didn't elaborate. 'What should I try first?'

'The lamb is a favourite of mine.' He gestured towards the plate. She moved towards it, inhaling the heady mix of fragrances the table conveyed. Contrary to his prediction, the food was only warm, not cold, which made it easier to taste. She scooped a small heaping of each onto her plate, only remembering she was naked when she sat down and her breasts pressed against the edge of the table. Heat flushed through her and she jerked her gaze to his to find him watching her intently.

She shovelled some food into her mouth to hide the flush of self-consciousness, and sharply forgot to feel anything except admiration for this meal. 'It's delicious,' she murmured, as soon as she'd swallowed.

'I'm glad you think so.'

'I don't know much about your country,' she

apologised. 'And I had no idea the food was so good.'

'There are two RKH restaurants in Manhattan,' he said with a lift of one brow.

'Really?'

He nodded. 'One off Wall Street and one in mid-town. This food came from the latter.'

'It wasn't prepared here?'

'No offence to your hotel staff, but RKH cooking is a slow process. Much done in the tagine, which takes hours. There are also a range of spices used that don't tend to be readily available in your kitchens.'

'Still, if we know in advance we can generally arrange anything.'

'RKH food cannot be easily faked.' He winked. 'Better to stick to chefs who prepare it as a matter of course, rather than try to imitate it.'

'You sound incredibly patriotic,' she murmured with a small grin.

'I'm the King—that's my job.'

'Right.' *The King.* A curse filled her brain as the enormity of what she'd done flooded her.

'Don't run away.' He spoke quietly, but with that same tone of command she'd heard from him a few times now. It was instinctive to him—a man who'd been born to rule.

'I'm…not.'

'You were thinking about it.'

She didn't bother denying it. 'It's just…you're a king. I can't…even imagine what your life is like.' She looked around the apartment, a small frown on her face. 'I guess it's like this, but on crack.'

'On crack?'

'You know, to the nth degree.'

He followed her gaze thoughtfully. 'My palace bears little resemblance to this apartment.'

'No?'

'For one thing, there is not a ceiling in the palace that is so low.'

A smile quirked his lips and her heart stammered. He was teasing her. She took another bite of the dinner, this time sampling the fish and okra. He was right. Now that she paid a little more attention, she could taste the difference. The spices were unusual—unlike anything she'd ever known. She doubted even the kitchens in this prestigious hotel could replicate these flavours.

'What is it like?'

'The palace?'

'The palace, the country. I know very little about where you're from,' she confessed. 'Only the basics I researched prior to your arrival.'

'Is this a normal part of your job?'

She nodded. 'I research what I think might

be necessary before any guest's arrival. Sometimes that's just their favourite foods or hotel habits, other times it's who they have restraining orders against.' She smiled. 'It depends.'

'And for me?'

Her stomach squeezed as she remembered looking at his photo on the Internet. Even then, she'd desired him. 'The basics,' she said vaguely. 'But nothing that told me of your country or your duties.'

He nodded, apparently satisfied. 'The RKH is one of the most beautiful places you could ever see. Ancient, but in a way that is visible everywhere you look. Our cities are built on the foundations of our past and we honour that. Ruins are left where they stand, surrounded by the modernity that is our life now. High-rise office buildings mingle with stone relics, ancient tapestries hang proudly in these new constructions—a reminder that we are of our past.'

A shiver ran down her spine, his language evocative. 'We are of our land, shaped by the trials of our deserts and the faraway ocean. Our people were nomadic for generations and our desert life is still a large pull, culturally. It is not unusual to take months out of your routine to go into the desert and live nomadically for a time.'

'Do you do this?'

'I cannot,' he admitted. 'Not for months at a

time, but yes, Daisy, for days I will escape the palace and move into the wild, untamed desert. There is something energising about pitting myself against its organic tests. Out there, I am just a man; my rank counts for nothing.'

His eyes dropped to her breasts and she felt, very strongly, that he was a man—all man. Desire slicked through her, and her knees trembled beneath the tabletop. She pushed some more food into her mouth, not meeting his eyes.

'Our people were peaceful for centuries, but globalisation and trade brought a new value to resources we took for granted. The RKH stands on one of the greatest oil sources in the world, and there are caves to the west that abound with diamonds and other rare and precious gems. The world's interest in these resources carried a toll, and took a long time to adapt to. We were mired in civil war for a hundred years, and that war led to hostilities with the west.' His face was tense; she felt the weight of his worries, the strength of his concern.

'My father was instrumental in bringing peace to my people. He worked tirelessly to contain our armed forces, to unify our military under his banner, to bring about loyalty from the most powerful families who had historically tilted for the rule of the country. He commanded loyalty.' He paused, sipping his water. 'He was…irreplaceable.'

She considered that. 'But peace has been long-established in the RKH. Surely you don't feel that there's a risk of war now?'

'There is always a risk of war,' he responded quickly, with a quiet edge to his voice. And she felt the weight of responsibility he carried on his shoulders. 'But I was raised to avert it. My whole life has been geared towards a peacemaking process, both within the borders of my land and on the world stage.'

'How does one man do that?'

He was reflective and, when he spoke, there was a grim setting to his handsome features. 'In many different ways.' He regarded her thoughtfully. 'Why didn't you become a concert pianist?'

The change of subject was swift but she allowed it. 'Reality intervened.' She said it with a smile, careful to keep the crushing disappointment from her voice—a disappointment that still had the power to rob her of breath.

'Oh?'

She took another bite of her meal—the last on her plate—and waited until she'd finished before answering. 'The Juilliard is expensive. Even on the partial scholarship I was offered, there's New York's cost of living.'

'And you couldn't afford it?'

Before Max, she could have. Easily. Her mother's inheritance had made sure of that. 'No.' A smile that cost her to dredge up. 'It was a pipe dream, in the end.'

He nodded, frowning, then stood. 'I asked you here tonight because I wanted to show you something.'

'Not because you wanted to drag me to bed?' She teased, glad to move the conversation to a more level ground.

'Well, that too.' He held a hand out to her. 'Come.'

It didn't even occur to her not to do as he said. She stood, putting her hand in his, aware of how well they fitted together, moving behind him, her near-nakedness only adding to her awareness of him. The Presidential suite was, as you might expect, enormous. In addition to the main living and dining area, there was a saloon and bar, furnished with the finest alcohol, a wall of classic literature titles, several in German and Japanese to cater to the international guests and now, a baby grand piano in its centre. Her heart began to speed for an entirely different reason now. Anxiety, longing, remorse. She lifted her gaze to him to find that he was watching her.

'That's a Kleshnër.'

He lifted a brow.

'The type of piano.' She moved towards it, as if drawn by an invisible piece of string. 'They're made in Berlin, only forty or so a year. They're considered to be the gold standard.' She ran her finger over the lid, the wood smooth and glossy. Her heart skipped a beat.

'Play something for me.'

She jolted her eyes to his.

'I want to hear you.'

She bit down on her lip, letting her finger touch the keys. How long had it been? Too long. Her insides ached to do as he said, to make music from ivory and ebony, to create sound in this room. But the legacy of her past held her where she was, the pain that was so intrinsic to her piano playing all bound together.

'You are afraid.'

The words inspired a complex response. She shook her head a little. 'Not really. It's just… been a very long time.'

His eyes narrowed speculatively, laced with an unspoken question. 'Play for me.'

She moved around behind the piano, staring first at the keys and then at his face, and it was the speculation she saw there that had her taking a seat behind the piano, her fingers hovering above the keys for several seconds.

'What would you like to hear?'

'Surprise me.'

She nodded again, and then, a small smile curved her mouth. 'This will be a first.'

'Oh?'

'Playing in only my underwear.'

His smile set flames alight inside her body. 'I could get you something, if you're cold, though I should tell you it is likely to decrease my enjoyment of your playing.'

'It's fine.' She winked. 'Just for you.'

He crossed his arms over his chest, waiting. She ran through a catalogue of songs, each of them embedded in her brain like speech and movement. Her fingers found the keys and she closed her eyes for a moment, breathing in deeply, straightening her spine, centring herself to the instrument, and then she began to play. Slowly at first, her interpretation of the Beethoven piece more tempered and gentle than many others. She kept her eyes closed as she played, the strength of the piece building inside her, and as she reached the midpoint and the tempo crescendoed, she tilted her head back, lost completely to the beauty of this form of communication.

The piece was not long—a little over four minutes. She played and when she hit the last notes, both hands pressed to the keys, she opened her eyes to find that the Sheikh had moved closer. He stood right in front of her, his eyes boring through her.

When he spoke, his voice was husky. 'Play something else.'

She lifted a brow, a teasing smile on her lips, but the look was somewhat undermined by the film of tears that had moistened her eyes.

'It's a beautiful instrument.' She ran her fingers over the keys. 'Did you have this brought up today?'

'I wanted to hear you.'

'A keyboard would have done.'

He shook his head. 'Show me something else.'

She did, this time, her favourite Liszt piece, the *étude* one she'd mastered only a week before her father had left home. She vividly recalled because she'd never got a chance to play it for him, and she had been practising so hard, preparing to surprise him with how she'd mastered the difficult finger movements.

'You play as well as you breathe,' he said softly, after she'd finished.

She blinked up at him, her eyes still suspiciously moist. When he pulled her to standing, she went willingly, and when he lifted her against his chest, carrying her back to bed, she felt only intense relief.

# CHAPTER FIVE

'YOUR HIGHNESS.'

The voice was coming to Daisy from a long way away. She shifted in bed a little, lifting a hand to run through her hair and connecting with something warm and firm. And it all came flooding back to her, so her eyes burst open and landed on a man she'd only ever seen in a professional capacity. Malik.

Oh, no!

She'd fallen asleep in the Sheikh's bed—she must have—and now it was morning and his suite was teeming with staff. It wasn't a particularly mature thing to do but she dragged the sheet up higher, covering her face, hiding from the servant.

'Privacy, Malik.' Sariq's voice was firm, and, yes, there was irritation there too.

'Yes, sir. Only you have a breakfast meeting with the President. The helicopter is ready to take you to Washington.'

'It will wait for me.'

'Yes, of course.'

A moment later, the door clipped shut.

'You can come out now.' His voice, so stern a moment ago, showed amusement now.

But it wasn't funny. She pushed at the sheet roughly, and her voice matched it. 'This is so not funny,' she said with a shake of her head, pushing her feet out of the bed and looking for her uniform. 'Oh, God. This is a disaster.'

His frown was way sexier than it should have been. 'Why?'

'Why? Because I told you, no one could know about this, and now that guy, Malik, has seen me *naked* in your bed! Oh, God.' She paced across the room, pulling her shirt on as she went, snagging a nail on one of the buttons and wincing.

'Malik can be trusted,' Sariq assured her.

'Says you, but what if he can't? What if he tells my boss?' She shook her head. 'I can't lose this job, Your Highness.'

At this, he barked a short, sharp laugh into the room. 'Your Highness? Daisy, I have made love to you almost the entire night. Can you call me Sariq now?'

She knew it was absurd, given that she'd already crossed a major professional line, but using his first name felt a thousand kinds of wrong.

'Daisy,' he insisted, moving out of bed, his

nakedness glorious and distracting and induc-
ing a panic attack because she'd slept with her
client—a lot—and now it was daylight and the
magic of the night before had evaporated and
she had to face the music. 'Relax. We are two
consenting adults who happen to have had sex.
This is not something you need to panic about.'

'You don't get it. I'm contractually forbidden
from doing this,' she muttered, his amusement
only making everything worse. 'It doesn't matter that we're consenting. You're off-limits to
me, or should have been.'

'It was one night,' he insisted calmly, coming to fold her in his arms and bring her to his
chest. 'Two nights, if you count tonight. And I
am counting tonight, Daisy, because I fully expect you to be here with me.'

'What if he tells—?'

He held a hand up imperiously, silencing her
with the single gesture. 'If Malik hadn't interrupted us, would you be feeling like this?'

She bit down on her lip, staring at him, and,
finally, shook her head.

'Good. Then this problem is easily solved. I
will order him to forget he saw you and it will
be done.'

She rolled her eyes. 'Nice try, but it's not actually that easy to remove a piece of someone's
memory.'

'Malik will do as I say. Put him out of your mind. I have.'

She looked up at him, doubts fading in the face of his confidence. 'I mean it,' she insisted. 'Tomorrow, you go back to your kingdom and nothing changes for you, but I need this job. My life has to go on as it did before, Sariq.' His name—the first time she'd said it—felt like magic. She liked the way it tasted in her mouth, and she especially liked the way he responded, the colour in his eyes deepening in silent recognition.

'And it will.' He dropped his head, his mouth claiming hers, so that thought became, momentarily, impossible. His kiss was heaven and his body weight pushed her backwards until she connected with the wall, so she was trapped between the rock hardness of him, and the wall, and her body was aflame with needs she knew she should resist.

But he lifted her, dispensing with the sheet and pressing her to the wall, his arousal nudging the heat of her sex, so she pushed down, welcoming him deep inside her as though it had been days, not hours, since they'd made love. His possession sent shockwaves of heat flaming through her and he hitched his hips forward and backwards, driving himself into her in a way that had her climaxing within a minute.

Her nails scored marks down his back and she almost drew blood from her lip with the effort of not screaming, in case he had other members of staff on the other side of the door.

It was the most sublime feeling, and whatever worries she had seemed far away now. He stilled, holding her, his expression taut, his arousal still hard inside her. She rolled her hips but he dug his hands into her flesh, holding her still.

'What is it?'

'I'm not wearing a condom.' He bit the words out, and she gasped.

'Oh, crap. I didn't even think…'

'Nor did I.' He lifted her from him, easing her to the ground gently, keeping his hands on her waist. 'Shower with me, *habibte*.'

Perhaps she should have declined, but she'd hours ago lost her ability to do what she ought and had abandoned herself, apparently, to doing only what she wanted.

'I suppose it is my job to cater to all your needs,' she purred, earning a small laugh from him. As she stepped into the shower and got the water going, she saw him remove a small foil square from the bathroom drawer and smiled to herself.

Half an hour later, still smiling, she blinked

up at him. 'Didn't Malik say the President was waiting?'

Sariq's eyes narrowed. 'He can wait.'

'Your betrothal is all but confirmed.'

Sariq fixed his long-term aide with a cool stare. 'And so?'

'The American—'

'Daisy.' He couldn't help the smile that came to him. Her name was so perfect for her, with her pale blonde hair and ready smile. 'Her name is Daisy.'

'The timing of this could be very bad, if it were to be in the papers in the RKH.'

'It won't be.'

'You are the Emir now, Sariq. More is expected of you than was a month ago. The affairs you once indulged in must become a part of your past.' Malik shook his head. 'Or if you must, allow me to engage suitable women for you, women who are vetted by me, by the palace, who sign confidentiality agreements and are certain not to sell their story to the highest bidder.'

'Daisy won't do that,' he murmured dismissively. 'And the days of palace concubines are long gone. I have no interest in reinvigorating that habit of my forebears.'

'Your father—'

'My father was a lonely man—' Sariq's voice held a warning '—who was determined to mourn my mother until the day he died. How he chose to relieve his bodily impulses is of little interest to me.'

'My point is that these things can be arranged with a maximum of discretion.'

'Daisy is discreet. There are three people who know about this, and it will stay that way.'

'If either of your prospective brides were to find out...'

Sariq tightened one hand into a fist on top of his knee, keeping his gaze carefully focussed on the view beneath him. The White House was just a spec in the distance now, the day's meetings concluded with success.

'They won't.'

'I don't need to tell you how important it is that your marriage settle any potential fallout from your father's death.'

Now, Sariq turned his head slowly, pinning his advisor with a steely gaze. 'No, you don't. So let it go, Malik. This conversation is at an end.'

'He's protective of me, of the kingdom. I've known him since I was a boy.'

Daisy lifted a hand, running the voluminous bubbles between her fingers. The warm bath water lapped at her breasts and, beneath the sur-

face, she brushed an ankle against his nakedness, heat shifting through her. Midnight had
come and gone and yet both were wide awake,
as though trying to cram everything into this—
their last night together.

'He won't say anything?'

'He's more concerned you will,' Sariq said
with a shake of his head.

'Me?' Daisy's brows shot up. 'Why in the
world…?'

'For money.' Sariq lifted his shoulders.

'Who would pay me for that information?'

His eyes showed amusement. 'Any number
of tabloid outlets? Believe it or not, my love life
is somewhat newsworthy.'

A shudder of revulsion moved down Daisy's
spine. 'You can't be serious?'

'Unfortunately, I am. Malik feels this indis-
cretion could be disastrous for my country, and,
in some ways, there's truth in that.'

'I'll try not to take that personally.'

'You shouldn't. It's not about you so much as
it is the women I'm supposed to marry.'

She froze. 'What?'

'I'm not engaged,' he reassured her quietly.
'And I will marry only one. But there are two
candidates, both daughters of the powerful
families who would have, decades ago, made
a claim for the throne. The thinking is that in

marrying one of them, I will unify our country further, bonding powerful families, allaying any prospective civil uprising.'

She absorbed that thoughtfully. 'Do you like these women?'

'I've met them a handful of times; it's hard to say.'

'You took me to bed after meeting me only a handful of times,' she pointed out.

'Then I like them considerably less than I like you,' he said, pushing some water towards her so it splashed to her chin.

She smiled back at him, but there was a heaviness inside her. 'What if you're not suited?'

'It's of little importance. The marriage is more about appearances than anything else.'

'You don't think you should care for your bride?'

Something darkened in his features and there was a look of determination there. 'Absolutely not.'

She shook her head. 'Why is that so ridiculous?'

'When it comes to royal marriages, arrangements of convenience make far more sense.'

'It's your life though. Surely you want to live it with someone that you have something in common with?'

'I will have something in common with my wife: she will love our country as I do, enough to marry a stranger to strengthen its peace.'

'And over time, you may come to love her?'

'No, *habibte*. I will never love my wife.' His eyes bore into hers. 'My father loved my mother and it destroyed him. Her death left him bereft and broken. I will never make that mistake.'

She was quiet. 'Do you think he felt it was a mistake to love her?'

'I cannot say. I think at times he wished he hadn't loved her, yes. He missed her in a way that was truly awful to watch.'

'I'm sorry.'

He shrugged. 'I have always known my own marriage would be nothing like his. If it weren't for the fact that I need a child—and as quickly as possible—then I would never marry.'

Something tightened in her chest—a fierce, primal rejection of that. In order to have children, to beget an heir, he would need to have sex, and, though she had no reason to presume he wouldn't, the idea of him going to bed with anyone else turned parts of her cold in a way she suspected would be permanent.

'Children? So soon?'

'I am the last of my family. It's not an ideal situation. Yes, I need an heir. My marriage will be organised within months.' His eyes assumed a more serious look. 'I have to leave here in the morning. I won't be back.'

Inexplicably, a lump formed in her throat. 'I know that.'

'And you, Daisy? What will your future hold? Will you stay working here, servicing guests of this suite of rooms for the rest of your life?'

Her lips twisted. 'I hope not.'

'The way you play the piano is mesmerising. You have a rare talent. It's wrong of you not to pursue it.'

Her smile was lopsided, his praise pulling at her in a way that was painful and pleasurable all at once. 'Like I said, it was a pipe dream.'

'Why?'

'My circumstances wouldn't allow me to study. Becoming a concert pianist isn't exactly something you click your fingers and do. It's hard and it's competitive and I had to get a job.'

'Why? When you had a scholarship...'

'I couldn't do it.'

He compressed his lips. 'If money was the only issue, then let me do as Malik suggested and offer you a settlement. He wanted me to ensure it was more profitable for you to keep your silence than not...'

She sent him a look of disbelief. 'I'm not going to tell anyone about this, believe me.'

'I know that. But I'd like to help you.'

'No.' She shook her head, tilting her chin defiantly. 'Absolutely not. You might be richer than Croesus but I'm not taking a cent from you, Sariq. I absolutely refuse.'

And while he might have been used to being obeyed, there was more than a hint of respect in his eyes when he met her gaze. 'Very well, Daisy. But if you should ever reconsider, the offer has no expiry date.'

She nodded, knowing she wouldn't. Once Sariq left, she would set about the difficult job of forgetting he ever existed. For her own sanity, she needed to do that, or missing him could very well be the end of her.

It was six weeks after he left that she put two and two together and realised the significance of the dates. A loud gasp escaped her lips.

'What is it?' Henry, beside her, turned to regard her curiously.

She shook her head, but the calendar on the counter wouldn't be silenced. She scanned through the guests she'd hosted in the last month and a half, since Sariq had left, and her pulse quickened.

Yes, she'd definitely missed a cycle. Instinctively, her hand curved over her flat stomach as the reality of this situation hit home.

She couldn't possibly be pregnant, though. They'd used protection. Every time? Yes, every time! Except that once, against the wall, but he hadn't climaxed, he'd been so careful. Surely that wasn't enough…

But there was no other explanation. Her cycle was as regular as clockwork; missing a period had to mean that somehow she'd conceived Sariq's baby.

She groaned, spinning away from Henry, uncertainty making it impossible to know what to say or do. First of all she needed proper confirmation.

'Do you mind if I clock out? I just remembered something.'

'Not at all. Make the most of the quiet days, I say.'

She bit down on her lip, grabbing her handbag. 'Thanks, Henry.'

There was a drugstore just down the block, but she walked past it, taking the subway across town instead. It was safer here, away from the possibility of bumping into anyone from the hotel. She bought three pregnancy tests, each from a different manufacturer, knowing that it was overkill and not caring, and a huge bottle of water, which she drank in one sitting. Once back at her small apartment in the basement of the hotel, she pulled a test from its packaging, taking it into the bathroom and following the instructions to the letter.

It took almost no time for two blue lines to appear on the test patch.

She swore under her breath, staring at the lines, a hardness filling out her heart.

What the heck could she do? Sariq had left America six weeks earlier. She hadn't heard from him and she had no expectation she would. He'd made it very clear that he needed to marry one of the women who would promise a greater hope of lasting peace for his people. He would make a match of duty, of national importance, and he'd need to have a legitimate heir with whomever he chose.

This baby would be a disaster for him, and, by extension, for his people. What if the sheer fact that she was pregnant somehow led to an all-out war in his country?

Nausea rose inside her. She cupped her hands over the toilet bowl, bending forward and losing all the water she'd hastily consumed. Her brow was covered in perspiration. She pressed her head to the ceramic tiles of the wall and counted to ten, telling herself it wasn't that bad, that things would work out. She could raise a child on her own. No one ever needed to know.

Daisy re-read the email for the hundredth time before sending it.

Sariq, I've reconsidered. Tuition for the Juilliard is in the attachment. Anything you can do to help…

There was nothing in there that could possibly give away the truth of her situation. No way would he be able to intuit from the few brief lines that there had been an unexpected consequence of their brief, passionate affair.

And that was what she wanted, wasn't it? To do this on her own? She bit down on her lip, her eyes scanning her phone screen, panic lifting through her. Because in all honesty, she couldn't have said *what* she wanted. Their baby, yes, absolutely. Already, she loved the little human growing inside her.

She'd begun to feel the tiniest movements, like little bubbles popping in her belly, and she'd known it was her son or daughter swimming around, finding their feet and getting stronger every day.

Time was passing too quickly. In only five months she'd have to stop working, and then what? Panic made her act. She needed help and Sariq had willingly offered it. Lying to him wasn't exactly comfortable for Daisy but she had to make her peace with that. Sariq had explained what he needed most—a wife and a legitimate heir to inherit his throne.

He'd be grateful to Daisy for this, in the long run, surely.

She read the email once more, her finger hovering over the 'send' arrow. She'd tried everything else she could think of. Thanks to her ex, her credit rating had tanked. She couldn't get a loan, and, even if she could, what in the world would she pay it back with?

For their child, she would do anything, even offer a tiny white lie, via email, to the man she'd had two passionate nights with months earlier. The end justified the means. The email made a whooshing sound as she finally sent it, but Daisy didn't hear it over the thunderous tsunami of her blood.

He stared at the email with an expression that was impossible to decipher. Three and a half months after leaving New York he had begun to think he would never hear from her again.

He re-read the email and a smile lifted his face. He had prayed she would come to her senses, but instinctively known not to push it. It wasn't his place to run her life. Daisy had to decide what she wanted. He wished he could give her more. He wished he could see her again. But knowing he could give her this small gift was enough.

Except it wasn't.

He awoke the next morning with a yearning deep in his soul and he had every intention of indulging it.

Malik was, naturally, against another trip to America.

'I am going,' Sariq insisted firmly, putting a hand on his advisor's forearm. 'Arrange the jet, call the embassy, notify them I'll be there for the weekend.'

'But, sir…'

'No, Malik. No. I'm doing this.'

He felt a thousand times lighter than he had the day before. It was only a temporary reprieve but, suddenly, seeing Daisy again felt like the right thing to do, and he was going to enjoy this last weekend before he made the official betrothal announcements.

Her email was a gift, and he had no intention of ignoring it.

# CHAPTER SIX

TO SAY THE building was imposing would be to say the sky was vast. She stared at the RKH embassy, just off Park Avenue, her heart hammering against her ribs.

I'm in Manhattan for the weekend. Come and see me.

A map had been attached to the email with directions to this building, and she'd been staring at it for the last twenty minutes, her central nervous system in overdrive as she tried to brace herself for this.

Keeping the truth of this from Sariq over email had been hard enough! But now? Keeping the secret from him when they were face to face? Daisy suspected it was going to take all the courage she possessed to go through with it.

Every instinct she possessed railed against it. She hated the idea! But what was the alternative? If she told him, then what? He'd be devastated.

She knew what was at stake for him, and why he needed to marry one of the women who would help him keep the peace in his country. The fact she'd fallen pregnant wasn't his fault and he didn't deserve to have to deal with this complication. More importantly, he wouldn't want to deal with it. He'd made that perfectly clear during their time together. It had been a brief passionate affair, nothing more. He'd gone back to the RKH and moved on with his life— the last thing he'd be expecting was the news that, actually, they'd made a baby together.

But didn't he have a right to know? This was his child. When she stripped away the fact he was a powerful sheikh, he was a man who had the same biological claim on this developing baby as she did. She made a noise of frustration, so a woman walking past stopped for a moment, shooting Daisy a quizzical look. She smiled, a terse movement of her lips, then turned away, drawing in a deep gulp of air. It tasted cold, or perhaps that was Daisy's blood.

The fact of the matter was, she couldn't strip his title away from his person. He wasn't just a man, he was a sheikh, and with his position came obligations she couldn't even imagine. One day, when he had the wife and heirs he'd explained to her were necessary, she might feel differently. Maybe then this child would be less of a problem for him. Maybe then he'd even want to know their son or daughter. But for now, she was better to assume all the responsibilities, to raise their child on her own.

It was the right decision, but she simply hadn't banked on how hard it would be to keep something of this magnitude a secret when she was going to see him. With him in the RKH, he was an abstract figure. While she dreamed of him at night and was startled by memories of his touch during the day, he was far away, and it was easy to believe he didn't think of her at all. For the sake of their child, she had to plan for her future knowing he wouldn't be a part of it.

Digging her nails into her palm and sucking in a deep breath for courage, she looked to the right and dipped her head forward as she crossed the street, approaching the embassy as though she were calm and relaxed when inside a wild kaleidoscope of butterflies had taken over her body.

Four guards stood on the steps, each heavily armed and wearing a distinctive army uniform. She swallowed as she approached the closest.

'Madam? What is it?' The guard studied her with an expression that gave nothing away.

'I have an appointment.' Her voice was soft.

She cleared her throat. 'His Highness Sariq Al Antarah asked me here.'

The guard's expression showed a hint of scepticism. 'What is your name?'

'Daisy Carrington.'

He spoke into a small receiver on his wrist and a moment later, a crackled voice issued onto the street. The guard nodded, and gestured to the door. 'Go on.'

Go on. So simple. If only her legs would obey. She stared at the shiny black doors, her pulse leaping wildly through her body, and concentrated on pushing one leg forward, then the next, until she was at the doors. On her approach, they swept inwards. More guards stood here but she barely noticed them at first, for the grandeur of this entranceway.

Walls and ceiling were all made of enormous marble blocks, cream with grey rippling through them. The floor was marble too, except gold lines ran along the edges. At several points along the walls there were pillars—marble— and atop them sat enormous arrangements of flowers, but unlike any she'd ever seen, vibrant, fragrant and stunning. She wanted to stop time and stare at them, to learn the names of these blooms she'd never seen before, to breathe each in and commit its unique scent to memory.

'Identification?' The guard's deep voice jolted her back to the present.

She held out her passport—it had been specified as the only suitable form of identification on the directions she'd received. Her passport had no stamps in it, and in fact she probably wouldn't have had a passport at all if it hadn't been necessary for the vetting process at the hotel.

The guard took it, opening it to the photo page and comparing the image to the real thing, then nodded without handing the passport back. 'Go through security.'

'My passport?'

'I need to make a copy.'

She frowned, uneasiness lifting in her belly. But Sariq was here, and so she wasn't afraid. She trusted him, and these were his people.

The security checkpoint was like any in an airport. She pushed her handbag and shoes through the conveyor belt then walked through an arch before collecting her things.

'His Highness is on the third floor,' a man to her right advised. He wasn't a security guard. At least, he wasn't wearing a military uniform. He wore robes that were white, just like Sariq's, but the detailing at his wrist was in cream. 'There is an elevator, or the central stairs.'

She opted for the latter. The opportunity to

observe this building was one she wanted to take advantage of. Besides, it would give her longer to steady her nerves and to brace herself for seeing Sariq again.

A hand curved over her stomach instinctively and she dropped it almost immediately. She had to be careful. No gestures that could reveal a hint of her condition.

The stairs were made of marble as well, but at the first floor, the landing gave way on either side to shining timber floors. The walls here were cream, and enormous pieces of art in gold gilt frames lined the hallway. There were more flowers, each arrangement as elaborate as the ones downstairs.

She bit down on her lip and kept moving. The next floor was just the same—polished timber, flowers, art, and high ceilings adorned with chandeliers that cast the early afternoon light through the building, creating shimmering droplets of refraction across the walls.

She held her breath as she climbed the next set of steps. This floor was like the others except there was a noticeable increase in security presence. Two guards at the top of the stairs, and at least ten in either direction, at each door.

'Miss Carrington?' A man in a robe approached her. She thought he looked vaguely familiar, perhaps from Sariq's stay at the hotel. 'This way.'

She fell into step beside him, incapable of speech. Anticipation had made it impossible. She was vividly aware of every system in her body. Lungs that were working overtime to pump air, veins that were taxed with the effort of moving blood, skin that was punctured by goose bumps, lips that were parted, eyes that were sore for looking for him.

At the end of the corridor, two polished timber doors were closed. There was a brass knocker on one. The man hit it twice and then, she heard him.

'Come.'

That one word set every system into rampant overdrive. She felt faint. But she had to do this. She hated having to ask him for money. She hated it with every fibre of her being, but what else could she do? She was already in a financially parlous state, but adding a baby to the mix and her inability to work? Neither of them would cope, and the comfort and survival of her child was more important than anything— even her pride.

The doors swung open and, after a brief pause, she stepped inside, looking around. The room was enormous. Large windows with heavy velvet drapes framed a view towards Bryant Park. She could just make out the tops of the trees from here. The furniture was heavy and wooden, dark leather sofas, and on the walls, the ancient tapestries Sariq had described. She took a step towards one, and it was then that she saw him.

Her heart almost gave way. She froze, unable to move, to speak, barely able to breathe.

Sariq.

Dressed in the traditional robes of his people, except in a more ornate fashion, this time he had a piece of gold fabric that went across his shoulders and fell down his front. On his head he wore the *keffiyeh*, and she stood there and stared at him dressed like this: every bit the imposing ruler. It was almost impossible to reconcile this man with the man who'd delighted her body, kissing her all over, tasting her, taking her again and again until she couldn't form words or thoughts. He looked so grand, so untouchable.

'Daisy.' Her name on his lips sent arrows through her body. She stayed where she was, drinking him in with her eyes.

'Your Highness.' She forced a smile to her lips, and was ridiculously grateful she'd taken care with her appearance. Her stomach was still flat but she'd chosen to wear all black—a simple pair of jeans and a flowing top, teamed with a brightly coloured necklace to break up the darkness of the outfit. She'd left her hair out and applied the minimum of make-up. His eyes dropped to her feet then lifted slowly over her body, so she felt warmth where he looked, as though he were touching her.

'I feel like I should curtsy or something.'

His look was impossible to decipher. 'That's not necessary.' He stayed where he was, and she did the same, so there was a room between them. The silence crackled.

'Thank you for seeing me,' she said, after a moment. God, this was impossible. She didn't want to ask him for money and, now that she saw him, the idea of having his baby and not telling him was like poison. All the very sensible reasons she'd used to justify that course of action fled from her mind.

He deserved to know. Even if he chose not to acknowledge the child? Even if he turned her away? Even if…the possibilities spun through her, each of them scary and real and alarming.

Her stomach was in knots, indecision eating her alive. She knew only one thing for certain: she had to decide what to do, and quickly. If she was going to tell him, it should be now. Shouldn't it?

She was every bit as beautiful as he remembered. More so. There was something about her today—she was glowing. Her skin was lustrous, her eyes shimmering, her lips, God, her lips. He wanted to pull them between his teeth, to drag her body to his and kiss her hard, to push her against the wall and make love to her as he'd done freely that weekend.

But that had been different somehow. They'd had an agreement. They'd known what they were to each other. Now? He was on the brink of announcing his marriage. Surely he couldn't still be fantasising about another woman?

But he was. He wanted Daisy. Not for one night, not for two. He wanted her for as long as he could have her.

*'Sire, you cannot see her again.'*

*Malik's warning had rung through the embassy.*

*'You were far from discreet last time. With your engagement due to be announced any day now, if word of this were to get out—'*

*'It won't. And I'm relying on you to make sure of that.'*

But Malik's reaction had been a good barometer. He was worried about Daisy, worried about what the people of the RKH would think if the affair became public, and with good reason. Sariq was no longer free to follow his passions wherever they took him. He was now the ruler. He'd been crowned, and the weight of a country rested on his shoulders.

He needed to remember that, and yet, faced with Daisy, he couldn't. He was not a man to throw caution to the wind. All his life he'd been trained for this, he knew what his responsibilities were, but suddenly he wondered if he could have his cake and eat it too.

His engagement hadn't been announced...yet. He had a little time. And he knew just how he wanted to spend it. He regarded her thoughtfully, something pulling at his gut, given how she was looking at him—as though she was remembering every single moment they'd shared, every kiss, whisper, pleasure.

He could postpone his trip, stay in New York a few more nights. Would she stay with him here, at the embassy? It was hard to read her, hard to know what she'd say if he suggested that. Besides, it wasn't enough. A few nights would satisfy him temporarily, but if the fourteen weeks since he'd last seen Daisy had taught him anything, it was that his need for her was insatiable, and not likely to be easily dispensed with. He wanted longer. As long as she could give him.

There was only one solution, and suddenly Sariq knew that if he didn't reach for it with both hands, he'd regret it for the rest of his life.

'I have a proposition for you. One I think you'll like.'

\* \* \*

She stood completely still except for her fingers, which she fidgeted behind her back. 'Oh?'

'Have a seat.' He gestured towards the dark leather sofas and she followed his gaze, but shook her head.

'I'd prefer to stand.'

'Would you like a drink?'

'No, thank you.'

He nodded.

'What is this proposition?'

'When is your admission set for the Juilliard?'

Darn it. She should have researched this. 'Mid-January,' she guessed, glad the words came out with such authority.

'In three months.' He ran a palm over his chin, as though contemplating this.

'Yes.'

'Then here is what I would like to propose. I want you to come to the RKH with me, Daisy.'

Her eyes flew wide and her lips parted. She stared at him, wondering if she'd imagined the words. 'But you're…aren't you getting married?'

He nodded. 'My situation is as it was before. I have chosen my bride, but the wedding date is not set.' Now he moved, closing the distance between them, until he was standing right in front of her. 'I will not marry her until you leave.'

A shiver ran down her spine, and she hated that heat was building low in her abdomen, filling her with a need that was instantly familiar even as revulsion gripped her, making her want to shout and stamp.

'No one could know you were there.' His jaw tightened, as though he were grinding his teeth. 'It would be a disaster if anyone were to find out, so we would have to be very, very careful.' He paused once more, and, for no reason she could fathom, Daisy held her breath. 'Malik would arrange it so that you were installed in an apartment in the capital. He would manage your security, ensure you were not seen by anyone but me. And I would visit you often.' He lifted a finger, tracing a line down her cheek towards her lips. She shivered again. 'It would be just like it was here, in New York. You would have a piano, and you would have me, and anything else you could want. And at the end of it, you would return to study, your tuition paid in full, a house provided for you in New York. Anything you wanted, Daisy.'

She stared at him, her heart dropping to her toes. Pain lashed her. What he was offering was little more than prostitution! Well? What had she expected? She'd come here, cap in hand, after the weekend they'd shared. Could he be blamed for thinking her attention could be bought? Her knees felt weak and her stomach hurt.

'You're asking me to come and be your secret mistress,' she repeated, incredulity ringing through her.

'I'm asking you to be my lover for as long as possible.'

'Before you get married.' She nodded, numb to the core.

He dipped his head in silent agreement.

'And in exchange, you'd give me money.'

Her insides lit up. Nausea crested through her.

'I will give you money anyway,' he assured her, as though just realising how mercenary the proposition sounded. She closed her eyes, wanting to blank him out for a moment, but even then, he was everywhere. His intoxicatingly masculine fragrance filled her. She was drowning in his presence and she desperately needed to think rationally and calmly.

'I cannot offer you more than this,' he said slowly, the words filled with the authority that came naturally to him, so she jerked her eyes open and looked at him once more. 'My duties to my country come first. I could never openly date you. A divorced American? My people wouldn't tolerate it. I know this isn't sensible. In fact, it's the opposite of that. If you were discovered, it would pose a real risk to my rule, but

I don't care. Daisy, I want you to come home with me. I want you to be my mistress more than I've ever wanted anything in my life.'

*A divorced American. His mistress!*

She felt so dirty! As though she was somehow lesser than him, and it brought back so many awful memories of her marriage, when Max had so cleverly undermined her confidence in herself until she saw her only value as being His Wife, rather than a person all her own. A shiver of revulsion ran down her spine, because she wasn't that woman any more.

'I can't believe you'd even suggest this.'

He moved forward, his body pressed to hers so weakness threatened to reduce her anger when she needed it most. 'How is it any different from that weekend?'

'You're getting married.'

'And I was getting married that weekend, too.'

'I had no idea the fact I was divorced and an American were such issues for you.'

He frowned, but it was swallowed quickly, as he dropped his head, his lips brushing hers. 'It isn't.'

'Not for your "mistress", anyway. I dare say someone like me is the perfect candidate for that role.'

His hands found the bottom of her shirt, lifting it so he could hold her bare hips, his lips more determined at hers now so a whimper filled her mouth and she felt herself kissing him back, needing him in a way that infuriated her.

'You are the perfect candidate to be in my bed, yes,' he agreed, but it hurt. God, it hurt. She'd never felt so...cheap.

She lifted her hands, pushing at his chest, putting some vital distance between them. 'Damn you, Sariq, no.' She shouted the words and then lowered her voice, aware that there were dozens of guards on this level. 'No.' A whisper. She wrapped her arms around her chest, moving away from him towards the sofas. Her knees were trembling but still she didn't sit. Her eyes were on him, showing her pain and hurt.

'I cannot offer you more than this,' he said again. 'You know what expectations are upon me. My marriage is a bargaining chip; my bride an important part of my political strategy. I cannot bring you to the palace as my mistress—it would offend my future Emira and it would offend my people. I'm sorry if this hurts you, but it is the truth.'

Her heart looped through her. Offend his bride. Offend his people. 'And what about me, Your Highness? Do you care that I am offended by this offer?'

He had the decency to look—for a brief moment—ashamed. But he rallied quickly, his expression shifting to a mask of determination. 'You shouldn't be. I'm offering us a way to both get what we want.'

She made a scoffing noise.

'Money aside, think about how good this could be. How much fun we'd have...'

She closed her eyes, the temptation of that warming her, because if she weren't so horrendously offended, she could see the appeal of his offer. On one level, he was offering her something she desperately wanted. More of Sariq? But everything about the way he'd made his offer filled her with disgust and loathing. He had somehow managed to cheapen what they'd shared so it felt tawdry and meaningless. And he didn't seem to get that!

'I thought you actually *liked* me,' she said with a small shake of her head. 'I thought you enjoyed spending time with me. That you valued me as a person.' Pain lashed her, because he didn't. He was just like her ex. The realisation was awful and horrifying.

'I do,' he promised immediately, crossing towards her. 'But I'm a realist and I see the limitations of this.'

'Which is sex,' she said crudely, lifting her brows, waiting for him to acknowledge it.

'As it was in New York,' he said firmly.

Her heart dropped. Her stomach ached and

tears filled her eyes. It had just been about sex for him? She wracked her brain, trying desperately to remember anything he'd said or done that indicated otherwise, but no. There was nothing. He'd wanted her. He'd made a point of saying that over and over, but that was all.

She'd been a fool to think there was more to it, that they were in some way friends or something.

'I shouldn't have come here. I shouldn't have asked you for money. It was a mistake. Please forget…'

'No.' He held onto her wrist as though he could tell she was about to run from the room. 'Stop.'

Her eyes lifted to his and she jerked on her wrist so she could lift her fingers to her eyes and brush away her tears. Panic was filling her, panic and disbelief at the mess she found herself in.

'How is this upsetting to you?' he asked more gently, pressing his hands to her shoulders, stroking his thumbs over her collarbone. 'We agreed at the hotel that we could only have two nights together, and you were fine with that. I'm offering you three months, on exactly those same terms, and you're acting as though I've asked you to parade naked through the streets of Shajarah.'

'You're ashamed of me,' she said simply. 'In

New York we were two people who wanted to be together. What you're proposing turns me into your possession. Worse, it turns me into your prostitute.'

He stared at her, his eyes narrowed. 'The money I will give you is beside the point.'

More tears sparkled on her lashes. 'Not to me it's not.'

'Then don't take the money,' he said urgently. 'Come to the RKH and be my lover because you want to be with me.'

'I can't.' Tears fell freely down her face now. 'I need that money. I need it.'

A muscle jerked in his jaw. 'So have both.'

'No, you don't understand.'

She was a live wire of panic but she had to tell him, so that he understood why his offer was so revolting to her. She pulled away from him, pacing towards the windows, looking out on this city she loved. The trees at Bryant Park whistled in the fall breeze and she watched them for a moment, remembering the first time she'd seen them. She'd been a little girl, five, maybe six, and her dad had been performing at the restaurant on the fringes of the park. She'd worn her Very Best dress, and, despite the heat, she'd worn tights that were so uncomfortable she could vividly remember that feeling now. But the park had been beautiful and her dad's music had, as always, filled her heart with pleasure and joy.

Sariq was behind her now, she felt him, but didn't turn to look at him.

'I'm glad you were so honest with me today.' Her voice was hollow. 'It makes it easier for me, in a way, because I know exactly how you feel, how you see me, and what you want from me.' Her voice was hollow, completely devoid of emotion when she had a thousand throbbing inside her.

He said nothing. He didn't try to deny it. Good. Just as she'd said, it was easier when things were black and white.

'I don't want money so I can attend the Juilliard, Your Highness.' It pleased her to use his title, to use that as a point of difference, to put a line between them that neither of them could cross.

Silence. Heavy, loaded with questions. And finally, 'Then what do you need such a sum for?'

She bit down on her lip, her tummy squeezing tight. 'I'm pregnant. And you're the father.'

# CHAPTER SEVEN

WHEN HIS MOTHER had died, Sariq had been speechless. Perhaps his father had expected grief. Tears. Anger. Something rent with emotion. Instead, Sariq had listened to the news.

*'She died, Riq. So did the baby.'*

He'd stood there, all of seven years old, his face like stone, his body slowing down so that blood barely pumped, heart barely moved, breath hardly formed, and he'd stared out of a window. Then it had been a desert view—the sands of the Alkajar range stretching as far as the eye could see, heat forming a haze in the distance that had always reminded Sariq of some kind of magic.

Now, he stared out at New York, streets that were crammed with taxis and trucks, the ever-present honking of horns filling him with a growing sense of disbelief. There were trees in the distance, blowing in the light autumnal breeze. His heart barely moved. His blood didn't pump. He could scarcely breathe.

Time passed. Minutes? Hours? He couldn't have said. He was conscious of the ticking of the clock—a gift from a long-ago American president to his father, on the signing of the Treaty of Lashar. He was conscious of the colour of her hair, so gold it matched the thread of his robes. The fragrance she brought with her, delicate and floral. He was conscious, somehow, of the beating of her heart. In contrast to his, it was firing frantically. It was beating for two people. Their unborn child was nestled in her belly, growing with every second that passed.

He closed his eyes, needing to block the world out, needing to block Daisy out in particular.

His breathing was ragged as he went back in time, calculating the dates. It had been what?— almost four months?—since his visit to America. When had she found out? And why had she waited until now to tell him?

Except, she hadn't come here to tell him.

His eyes flared open and flew to her with renewed speculation and his heart burst back to life, pushing blood through his body almost too fast for his veins to cope. The torrent was an assault.

'You weren't going to tell me.'

A strangled noise was all the confirmation he

needed. He stood perfectly still, but that was no reflection of his temperament or feelings.

'You came here today to collect a cheque. If I hadn't suggested you join me in the RKH, you would have taken the money and left. True?'

She didn't turn to face him and suddenly that was infuriating and insupportable. He gripped her shoulders and spun her around. Tears sparkled on her lashes and his gut rolled, because he hated seeing her like this but his own shock and anger and disbelief made it impossible for him to comfort her.

'This baby is a disaster for you.'

She was right. His eyes swept shut once more as he tried to make sense of the political ramifications of having conceived a child with a divorced American—a woman he spent approximately forty-eight hours of his life with, if that.

'I didn't come here to tell you, because I understand your position. You have to get married and have children with someone who will strengthen your position, not weaken it. This baby was a mistake.' Her face paled. 'No, not a mistake,' she quickly corrected, her hand curving over her stomach so his eyes dropped to the gesture, something different moving through him now. Was that joy? In the midst of this? Surely not.

'A surprise,' he substituted, his voice gravelled by the emotions that were strangling him.

'You could say that.' Her short laugh lacked humour.

'So what was your plan?'

'Plan?' She bit down on her lip. 'I wouldn't say I have a plan.'

'You came to take money from me under false pretences? And then what?' It was unreasonable, and not an accurate representation of how he felt. He wasn't sure why he had chosen to hone in on that. The money was beside the point, but her duplicity wasn't.

She flinched but nodded, as though his accusation had some kind of merit. 'Believe me, I hate that I came here with my hand out. I hate having to ask you for anything. But I can't afford a child, Sariq. I can't afford this.' Tears ran down her cheeks now and his chest compressed almost painfully.

'The hotel doesn't pay you well?'

'My salary's fine.' She dashed at her tears, her eyes showing outrage. Outrage that she was crying. Outrage that she had to explain her situation to him. But he needed to understand…

'I lost a lot of money in my divorce. I have a mountain of debt with interest rates that are truly eye-watering. My salary lets me chip maybe five thousand dollars a year off the total owed. I should be out from under that in about, oh, I don't know, seventy or eighty years?' She shook her head. 'I can't afford to stop working. The hotel provides my accommodation so once I stop working, I'll need to find somewhere to live, which I can't afford. Benefits won't cut it. I hate that I'm asking you for money,' she repeated, and he felt it, every single shred of her hate and fury and fear, too. 'But we're having a baby and I need to do what I can for her or him.'

'Yes.' It was an immediate acquiescence. He turned away from Daisy, stalking towards the door, staring at it for a moment. His mind was spinning at a thousand miles per hour. His marriage was important. Unifying his country further mattered. But so did begetting an heir. His situation as the last in his family's line had troubled him for a long time, but never more so than since losing his father. He was conscious of how much rested on his survival, how vulnerable that made him. And if there was one thing he hated, it was feeling vulnerable.

This child alleviated that.

He had an heir—or he would, in six months' time.

'Look at me, Sariq.' Her voice cut through him, the grief there, the pain. He turned and his heart jolted inside him, because she was clearly terrified. If he stopped for a moment and saw this from her perspective, he could see how unsettling the discovery of her pregnancy must have been. Neither of them had wanted complications from that weekend. It had been a stolen time of passion, short and brief. And definitely over.

But it wasn't.

This baby would bind them for ever.

'I can't afford to do this on my own, and I hate that, but the alternatives don't bear considering.' A shiver moved her slender frame. Her too-slender frame. Had she *lost* weight since he'd seen her last?

A frown pulled at his mouth. 'You're slim.'

She blinked, the statement apparently making no sense.

'You haven't gained weight. In fact, the opposite appears to be true.'

'Oh.' She nodded jerkily. 'Yes. I haven't felt well. The doctor at the free clinic says that will probably pass soon enough.'

His frown deepened. He didn't feel that was it. Was it possible that she hadn't been eating? That she hadn't been eating well enough? Because she was worried about money?

And as for a *free clinic*? She was carrying the sole heir to the throne of the RKH, one of the most prosperous countries in the Middle East—and the world! She should have top-level medical care. He needed to fix this—he needed to find a way to make this work, for everyone.

'The baby's healthy,' she said quietly. 'I'm fine, apart from the all-day nausea and complete lack of appetite.'

He nodded slowly, fixing his eyes to her. There was only one solution, and he needed it to happen immediately. 'I'm glad you came to me today, Daisy. I'm glad you told me.'

She let out a whoosh of breath, her relief apparent. 'You are?'

A simple nod. 'But we must move quickly in order to avoid a major diplomatic incident.'

She blinked. 'Oh, I'm not going to tell anyone about this, Your Highness.'

He laughed then, a deranged sound. 'For God's sake, we've conceived a child together. We're going to be parents. Call me Sariq.'

She bristled, her eyes showing strength and determination. 'We are *not* going to be parents together.' She spoke with a cool authority that was belied by the quivering of her fingers. 'You're going to be in another country, far away. I'm going to raise our child.'

His eyes narrowed imperceptibly. 'You know what this baby means to me.'

She froze.

'You know how imperative it is that I have an heir.'

'But this baby *isn't* your heir,' she mumbled after a moment. 'We're not married. It can't be…'

'We're not married, *yet.*'

Her eyes flared wide in her beautiful face, and her lips dropped to reveal her glossy white teeth. She didn't speak. She couldn't. Good. He needed a moment to organise this. He crossed to his desk, picking up the phone. 'Have Malik call me.'

He disconnected the receiver once more and turned to face her. She was standing where he'd left her, shaking her head.

'Sit down, *habibte.*'

She shook her head harder. 'I'm not marrying you.'

Determination flooded him as he saw the only path before them clearly, and knew he had to guide them down it. 'There is no alternative, Daisy, so I suggest you move past shock to acceptance. The sooner you do so the better, for both of us.'

She stared at him, her insides awash with uncertainty and disbelief. 'You can't be serious?'

'Does it sound like something I'd joke about? This child has more value to my people and me than I can possibly describe. You are carrying my royal heir. There is no option but for us to marry.'

'I beg your pardon,' she spat, crossing her arms over her chest, wishing his eyes didn't drop to her cleavage in that way that reminded her of everything they'd shared that weekend. 'There is one option, and it's the one we're going to take. I'm going to leave here now, with a cheque that will help me cover medical expenses and rent in some kind of home in which to spend the first year of our child's life, until I can go back to work—'

'Go back to work?' His laugh was a caustic sound of derision. 'And who will be raising the crown prince of the RKH?'

'Or princess,' she snapped caustically. 'And I don't know. I'll find a family day care.'

'Family day care?' he repeated, and she nodded, though she could understand his reaction to that. It was a little haphazard and ill-thought-out.

'I don't know, okay? I haven't gotten that far. I just know that I can do this on my own.' She lifted her chin, breathing in deeply in an attempt to calm her nerves. 'I haven't told anyone anything about what happened between us and I don't intend to. I won't say a word about the fact you're this baby's father. Your name won't appear on the birth certificate. It will remain untraceable.'

His jaw clenched. 'You think this will please me? For my own child not to bear my name?'

His nostrils flared with the force of his exhalation. 'Honestly, Daisy, your naivety would almost be adorable if it weren't so inappropriate.'

Anger flared inside her. 'I beg your pardon?'

'How hard do you think it would be for someone to piece this together?' He held her gaze with obvious contempt. 'You cannot imagine the scrutiny my life is subject to. You are acting as though I am any other man, as though this child is like any other love child.'

'I'm sorry, it's my first time being pregnant after a one-night stand,' she muttered sarcastically. 'I have no idea how I'm supposed to act.'

'You're supposed to be reasonable,' he responded flatly. 'There is no way I'm having my child raised anywhere besides my palace and I think you knew that when you told me about your pregnancy.'

His words hit her like a mallet. She shook her head again, feeling like one of those bobble-head dolls.

'Listen to me, Daisy.' He began to move closer to her so she braced instinctively. Not out of fear of him so much as fear of her reaction. How, even in that moment, could she be aware of trivial matters such as the breadth of his shoulders and the strength of his arms?

'I need an heir. You know this, and you understand why it's an urgent concern. As the last remaining heir of my family's line, I am in a vulnerable position…'

She jerked her head in an aggressive nod. 'Which is why you're marrying and planning to have a child as soon as—'

'I have a child.' The words cut through the room, loud and insistent. He paused, visibly calming himself. 'We are having a child.' And now, he closed the distance, gripping her hands and lifting them between them, his eyes boring into hers with the force of a thousand suns.

'You're wrong. I didn't come here to tell you about this. I understand your position, which is precisely why I intended to do this on my own. You don't want to marry me. You don't want to raise a child with me. Your people need you to do what's best for them, and that includes marrying a woman who will secure the peace of your kingdom. I can't do that.' She was trembling, she realised belatedly. He squeezed her hands tighter. 'I won't marry you.' Oh, no. Her teeth were chattering. Panic was setting in.

'You must.'

'No.' Fear strangled her words. 'I've already been married, and it was a disaster. I swore I'd never do that again. I can't.' Tears fell from her eyes. How angry they made her! How frustrated with herself she felt. This was not a time to cry!

She ripped her hands free and wiped at her

face, hard, turning away from him and grabbing her handbag. She didn't even remember discarding it but she must have placed it on the chair near the door when she'd entered this room, because it sat there, looking at her in a matter that felt accusatory.

'I want you to forget I came here.'

'I can't do that.'

She spoke as though he hadn't. 'I want you to forget I'm pregnant. No, I want you to forget we ever met.'

'You are not leaving here.'

'Oh, yeah?' She pushed the strap of her bag over her shoulder and whirled around to face him. She felt like a wild animal, all emotion, no civility. 'Try and stop me.'

'I do not need to try to stop you.' He was so infuriatingly calm! It only flared her anger further. 'Have you forgotten where you are, *habibte*?'

'I'm in New York City. You might be King of all you survey in the RKH, but here in America we believe in the rule of law, which means no one, regardless of their position or station, has more legal rights than another.'

'I know what the rule of law is.' He crossed his arms over his chest. 'I'm sorry to say it won't help you here.'

It was like being hit with a sledgehammer.

Cold, claw-like fingers began to wrap around her as the enormity of her own stupidity hit her like an anvil.

She wasn't in America any more. Not really. She'd willingly stepped into his embassy, buried herself in the thick of dozens of his guards and surrendered her passport.

'Oh, my God.' She stared at him, her face heating to the point of boiling, her eyes showing her comprehension. 'You…bastard.'

His head jerked a little, as though she'd slapped him.

'You tricked me.'

His eyes flashed with impatience. 'I did no such thing. I invited you here because I wanted to see you again—'

'To proposition me,' she corrected witheringly, but her voice shook, panic making it impossible to speak clearly, much less think straight. 'That's why you lured me here to your embassy?'

And despite the tension, he laughed, and it did something to her insides, reminding her of the warmth they'd shared, of his easy affection. Her stomach squeezed and she reached behind her, feeling for the chair that had, until a moment ago, held her handbag.

'Do you think I have to resort to kidnap in order to get a woman into my bed?'

His eyes lanced her and she felt angry, stupid and jealous as all heck, all at once.

He softened his tone. 'And I didn't lure you here. This is where I live when I'm in the States. Up until a month ago, it was being renovated and wasn't fit for habitation, hence I stayed at your hotel. As it's now restored to its usual condition, I'm here. This was not a trap.'

'It sure feels like it.'

He dipped his head forward in silent acceptance of that. 'I'm sorry.' His eyes pinned to hers and she was powerless to look away. He strode across the room, crouching before her, clasping her hands in her lap. 'I am sorry.' His expression showed the truth of his words. 'I'm sorry I didn't prevent you from falling pregnant. I'm sorry that my position makes our marriage a necessity. But I am sorriest of all for the fact that I cannot take the time to slowly convince you this is the right thing for us to do. I cannot risk letting you walk out of here because we *must* marry. It is imperative.' He stroked her hand and her heart ached, because she wasn't sure how she felt and what she wanted but she could see, so clearly, what this meant to him and his people.

But what about her and her needs? Memories of Max had her shaking her head from side to side, needing him to understand. 'I don't want to get married. I can't.'

'I understand that. Put that to one side for the moment and think about our child.' His hand shifted, moving from her wrists to her stomach, pressing against it, and for a moment he appeared to lose his train of thought as he lost himself in the realisation that inside her belly was their own baby.

'Don't you think our child deserves this?'

She bit down on her lip. 'Our child deserves us to love it,' she said quietly. 'To do the best for it, always.'

'And raising him or her together is the best.'

'My mother raised me on her own after my father left,' she insisted, tilting her chin with pride for the job her mother had done even when she'd struggled with her health for years.

'I didn't know that.'

'Why would you? We don't know each other, Sariq. We don't know each other.'

'Don't we?' The question laid her bare and forced her to look inside herself. They might not know one another's biographical details back to front, but she would have said that despite that, after their time together, she *did* know him. But that he was capable of this? Of holding her prisoner in his embassy?

It renewed her anger and disbelief, so she

stood a little shakily, moving towards the door. 'You're not going to keep me prisoner here until I agree to marry you.'

'No,' he acquiesced, and relief burst through her. 'We are getting married this evening, Daisy. There is no point fighting over the inevitable.'

He watched her from the mezzanine, and he felt many things. Desire. Shock. Certainty. Admiration. But most of all, he felt a sense of guilt. Her displeasure with this was understandable. She'd arrived at the embassy with no concept of how he would react, and he'd wielded his power like a sledgehammer.

He hated this.

He hated what he was doing, he hated that he was doing it to Daisy, and yet he knew he had no alternative. Not only was their child incredibly politically powerful, if he didn't marry her and bring her to the RKH there was a very real threat to both of them. Only in his palace, with the royal guards at his disposal, could he adequately protect them.

He hadn't wanted to hit her over the head, metaphorically speaking, with the truth of that. It felt like the last thing you should say to a pregnant woman, and yet undeniably there were some factions within his country who would strike out at his heir. And particularly an illegitimate yet rightful heir who could, at any point, return to the RKH and claim power.

For years, he'd believed his mother had died in childbirth. His father had wanted it that way. But when Sariq was fifteen, he'd learned the truth. She'd been murdered. When she was heavily pregnant, while on a private vacation, someone had killed her. Sariq should have been there. He was part of the plan, too, but at the last moment he'd come down with a virus and his father had insisted he stay home to avoid making his mother sick in her delicate state.

He knew, better than anyone, what some factions were capable of and there was no way he was seeing history repeat itself. He would protect Daisy and their unborn child with his dying breath.

No, he had to do this, even when it left a sour taste in his mouth. As to her suitability? He had no doubts on that score; she'd be a fish out of water at first. Who wouldn't? She wasn't raised with these pressures; she had no concept of what would be expected of her. She'd never even travelled outside America, for Christ's sake. His advisors would question his judgement, and they'd be right to do so. There would be political ramifications, but he was counting on the spectre of a royal baby on the horizon to quell those.

At the end of the day he had made his decision and there was no one on earth who could shake him from his sense of duty and purpose. She was angry now, but once they arrived in the RKH and she saw the luxury and financial freedom that awaited her, surely that would ease? In time, when she realised that their marriage was really in name only, a legal arrangement, more than anything, to bind them as parents and to right their child's claim to the throne.

And the fact he couldn't look at her without wanting to tear her clothes from her body?

It was irrelevant. He had a duty to marry her, to protect her with his life. Everything else was beside the point.

## CHAPTER EIGHT

THE DRESS WAS STUNNING. It was perfect for a princess. A pale cream with beads that she was terrified to discover were actual diamonds, stitched around the neckline, the wrists and at the hem, so that the dress itself was heavy and substantial. It nipped in at her waist to reveal the still-flat stomach. On her feet she wore simple silk slippers, for which she was grateful— the last thing she wanted was to be impeded by high heels.

They'd make it far more difficult to run away.

Except she wasn't going to run away. She caught her reflection in the windows across the room. Evening had fallen, meaning she could see herself more clearly. And more importantly, New York was gone. There were lights, in the distance, and the tooting of cars, but the trees of Bryant Park were no longer visible. She lifted a finger to her throat, toying with the necklace her mother had given her, running the simple silver locket from side to side distractedly.

There were guards everywhere. Escape wasn't an option. But even if it were, Daisy wasn't sure she would take it. She knew there were many, many single parents out there doing an amazing job, and perhaps if Daisy hadn't already been worn down by extreme poverty, hunger, and the fear of living pay cheque to pay cheque, she might have had more faith in her abilities. But the truth was, she knew what it was like to be poor, to be broke, to have enormous debts nipping at her heels, and she wanted so much more for her baby.

It wasn't just the financial concerns though. It was the certainty that if she didn't marry Sariq she would need to go back to work as soon as possible, and already she hated the idea of leaving her baby.

Still, marriage felt extreme.

So why wasn't she fighting? Insisting that she be allowed to call a lawyer?

Was it possible that on some level she actually wanted this? That her body's traitorous need for his was pushing her towards this fate, even when she wanted to rail against it?

She couldn't say. But she knew a thousand and one feelings were rushing through her and not all of them were bad. Which made her some kind of traitor to the sisterhood, surely?

She ground her teeth together, looking around this enormous space idly until her eyes landed on a figure on the mezzanine level and she froze.

'Sariq.' His name escaped her lips without her consent. Then again, it was preposterous to keep calling him by his title. He was watching her like a hawk, his eyes trained on her in a way that made her stomach clench with white-hot need, so fierce it pushed her lips apart and forced a huge breath from her body. She spun away, ashamed of her base reaction. A moment later, he had descended the steps and was behind her, his hands on her shoulders, turning her to face him.

He didn't speak. His eyes held hers, and he studied her for several seconds. 'Are you ready?'

Her heart began to tremble. 'If I said "no", would it make any difference?'

He eyed her for several seconds. 'Yes.'

Her pulse raced. Disappointment was unmistakable and that only made her angrier.

'So you'll let me go?'

'No.' He shook his head. 'But I will delay. We can wait a day or two to let you get used to this. We can talk until you understand. I can prepare you better for what's in store once we arrive in the RKH…'

'But you won't let me leave this embassy?'

Silence prickled between them. 'I cannot.'

'Then I see no point in delay, except to assuage your conscience, which I have no intention of doing.'

He stared at her, surprise obvious on his features. She knew she was lashing out at him out of fear, and that it wasn't fair. He had been as caught off guard by this as she was. He was acting out of duty for his country, and she understood that. But becoming a commodity didn't sit well with her, and her desire for him was making everything else murky and uncertain.

'You're forcing me to marry you, Sariq. I'm not going to let you think otherwise.' His face paled beneath his tanned skin, and she was glad. Hurting him, arousing his conscience, made her feel a hell of a lot better. She struck again: 'You should know that. I'm marrying you because I have to—not because I want to—and I will never forgive you for this. Tonight I'm going to become your wife and I may appear to accept that, I may appear to accept *you*, but I will always hate you for this.' She glared at him with undisguised fury so it was easy for Sariq to believe her. 'I love our child, and, for him or her, I will try to make our marriage amicable, at least on the surface, but don't you ever doubt how I really feel.'

His eyes swept shut for a moment, the only movement on his stone-like face the furious beating of a muscle in his jaw. 'I wish we had an alternative.'

'You do,' she said quietly.

His eyes glittered with something like fire and he reached into his robes, removing a phone. It was a familiar brand but the back was pure gold. He loaded something up on the screen then handed it to her.

She stared at it, her own photo looking back at her, beside his picture, and beneath a headline that screamed *Secret Royal Wedding!*

She read the article quickly.

*News broke overnight that the Emir of the Royal Kingdom of Haleth married American Daisy Carrington when he was last in the United States in July.*

*The wedding, conducted in secret, means the unknown woman is now Emira to one of the world's most prosperous nations.*

*Little is known of the woman who stole the famously closed-off ruler's heart, or of how their romance began.*

*More details to follow.*

'We're not married.' She handed the phone back to him, wishing her fingertips weren't trembling.

'Our marriage certificate will be backdated, to remove any doubts as to my paternity.'

Her eyes narrowed. 'This is your child.'

'I know that.' He pocketed his phone once more. 'I have no doubt on that score. It makes things easier, that's all.'

'But…'

'Your name is in the papers, Daisy.' There was urgency in his tone. 'The whole world will know that you are carrying my baby before the morning. And that baby is the heir to my throne. Can you not see how vulnerable that makes you both?'

She stared at him in disbelief, and desire died, just like that. Now, her feels were not unambiguous at all. Anger sparked through her, overtaking everything else.

'You are such a bastard. You did this on purpose, so I'd go through with this?'

'I didn't need to,' he murmured. 'Our marriage is a *fait accompli*.'

'But this is insurance,' she insisted. 'Because if I somehow managed to walk out of here, my life would never be the same again, right?'

He didn't respond. He didn't need to. He'd manoeuvred her into a position that made her agreement essential. She wasn't as naïve as he seemed to think. She knew what this baby would mean for her, she knew that there'd be a stream of paparazzi wanting to capture their child's first everything, following her around mercilessly.

'I need you both in the RKH where I can protect you.' He spoke simply, the words so final they sent a shiver down her spine. 'I'm sorry for the necessity of this, but I am not prepared to take any chances with your life.'

'You're being melodramatic.'

His eyes narrowed. 'My mother was killed by terrorists. She was eight months pregnant. I was supposed to be with her that day.' Each sentence was delivered with a staccato-style finality but that didn't make it any easier to digest. 'I will not let anyone harm you.'

Her heart slowed down. Pity swarmed her and, despite the situation she found herself in, she lifted a hand and pressed it to his chest. 'I'm so sorry, Sariq. I had no idea.'

He angled his face away, his jaw clenched. 'It was kept quiet. My father was determined to maintain the peace process and so news was released that she died in childbirth.' His features were like granite. 'The perpetrators were found and convicted in a court convened for the purpose of conducting the trial away from the media's eyes.'

She sucked in a breath, with no idea what to say. A shiver ran down her spine. She was deeply sorry for him, for the boy he'd been and the man he was now, and yet she had to make him see things were different. 'I'm in America, not the RKH, and if you hadn't released this, no one would even know who I am.'

'You underestimate the power and hatred of these people.' He lifted a hand, touching the back of his fingers to her cheek so lightly that she had to fight an impulse to press into his touch.

'But no one knew me.'

'They would have found you. Both of you. Believe me.'

His hand dropped to her stomach. 'I know we each want what is best for our child, Daisy.'

He was right. On that point, they were in total agreement.

'Tell me what you want from me, when we are married,' he said quietly. 'What will make this easier for you?'

It was an attempt at a concession. She bit down on her lip, with no idea how to answer. The truth was, she really couldn't have said. She had so many questions but they were all jumbling around her head forming a net rather than a rope, so she couldn't easily grasp any single point.

'I just need space,' she said simply. 'Once we're married, I need you to leave me alone and let me get my head around all this. And then, we'll have this conversation.'

He looked as though he wanted to say something but then, after a moment, he nodded. 'Fine. This, I can do.'

Daisy's head was spinning in a way she doubted would ever stop. From the short wedding ceremony at the embassy to a helicopter that had flown them to a private terminal at JFK, to a plane that was the largest she'd ever been on that was fully private. It bore the markings of the RKH and was, inside, like a palace. Just like the embassy, it was fitted with an unparalleled degree of luxury and grandeur. A formal lounge area with large leather seats opened into a corridor on one side of the plane. Sariq had guided Daisy towards it and then gestured to the first room. 'My office, when I fly.' A cursory inspection showed a large desk, two computer screens and a pair of sofas.

'A boardroom, a cinema,' he continued the inventory as they moved down the plane. 'A bathroom.' But not like any plane bathroom she'd ever been on. Then again, they'd been short domestic flights from one state to the next, never anything like this. A full-sized bath, a shower, and all as you'd find in a hotel; nothing about it screamed 'airline'.

'Here.' He'd paused three doors from the end of the plane. 'It's a twelve-hour flight to Shajarah. Rest.'

She'd looked into the room to see a bed—king-size—made up sumptuously with cream bed linen and brightly coloured cushions. She still wore the dress in which she'd said her wedding vows—in English, out of deference to her, but at the end in the language of Haleth. She'd stumbled while repeating the words and her cheeks had grown pink and her heart heavy at the enormity of what was ahead of her. She would need to learn this language, to speak it with fluency, to be able to communicate with her child, who would grow up hearing it and forming it naturally.

'I'm not tired.'

Except she was. Bone tired and overwhelmed.

'There are clothes in there.' He gestured towards a small piece of furniture across the room, but made no effort to leave her. His eyes were locked to hers and her pulse began to fire as feelings were swamped by instinct and she wanted, more than anything, to close her eyes and have things go back to the way they used to be between them. She remembered the feeling of being held by him, his strong arms wrapping around her and making her feel whole and safe. But there was no sense seeking refuge from the man who had turned her life upside down.

'Thank you.' A prim acknowledgement. She stepped into the room, looking around, then finally back to facing him. Just in time to see him pull the door closed—with him on the other side of it.

Alone once more, she still refused to give in to the tears that had been threatening her all day. She blinked furiously, her spine ramrod straight as she walked across the room, pulling open the top drawer of the dressing table and lifting out the first thing she laid her hands on. It was a pair of pants, and, despite the fact they were a comfortable drawstring pair, they were made of the finest silk. Black, they shimmered as she held them, and at their feet there was a fine gold thread, just like the robes he wore. A matching shirt was beneath the pants. With long sleeves and a dip at the neck, it was like wearing water—so comfortable against her skin that she sighed. The engines began to whir as she pulled the blankets back and climbed into bed. She was asleep before the plane took off.

Daisy would have said she was too tired to sleep, but she slept hard, almost the entire way to the RKH. She might have kept sleeping had a perfunctory knock at the door not sounded, wrenching her from dreams that were irritatingly full of Sariq. His smile when they'd talked, his laugh when she'd made a joke. His eyes on her in that way of his, so thoughtful and watchful, intent and possessive, so her blood felt like lava and her abdomen rolled with desire.

And then, the man himself stood framed in the door of her room and her dreams were so tangible that she almost smiled and held a hand out to him, pulling him towards her. Almost. Thank goodness sanity intervened before she could do anything so stupid.

'Yes?' The word was cold. Crisp. He didn't react.

'In two hours, we will land. There is some preparation you will need to undergo, first.' His eyes dropped lower, to her décolletage, and she was conscious of the way the shirt dipped revealing her flesh there, showing a hint of her cleavage. 'You must be hungry.'

The last words were said in a voice that was throaty.

'I'm not.'

Disapproval flared in his features but for such a brief moment that it was gone again almost immediately, so she thought she'd imagined it. 'Come and join me while I eat, then.'

'A command, Your Highness?'

Silence. Barbed and painful. Her stomach squeezed. 'If that's what it takes.' He looked at her for a moment longer. 'Two minutes, Daisy.'

He pulled the door shut before his frustration could become apparent. But he *was* frustrated. In his entire life, he'd never known someone to be so argumentative just for the sake of it. Sariq was used to being obeyed at all times, yet Daisy seemed to enjoy countermanding his words.

And when they were in the RKH? While the country was famously progressive in the region, there was no getting away from the fact it was still patriarchal and mired in many of the ways of the past. Her flagrant flouting of his wishes would raise questions he'd prefer not to have to answer.

Couldn't she see that their situation required special handling? It was as undesirable to him as it was to her—but what choice did either of them have? She was carrying his child, the heir to the RKH. This marriage, living together as man and wife, was the only solution to that situation.

He had to make her understand the difficulties inherent to her situation without terrifying her. He pressed his back against the door, closing his eyes for a moment, so that he saw his father again and a darkness filled him. He didn't want to think about what his father might say about this. Sariq was Emir now. The safety and prosperity of the kingdom lay on his shoulders, and his alone.

Alone again, Daisy flopped onto her back and stared at the ceiling, his command wrapping around her, making breathing difficult. She wasn't hungry, but she was thirsty—the thought of coffee was deeply motivating—and yet she stayed where she was, an emptiness inside her. And she knew why.

The Sariq of her dreams had been the man she'd fallen into bed with, the man who had bewitched and made her feel alive for the first time since Max. But he was gone, and there was only this Sheikh in his place. All command and duty. The juxtaposition was inherently painful.

She bit down on her lip, not moving, the emptiness like a black hole, carrying mass of its own, weighing her down, holding her to the bed. She lay there for a long time, certainly past the allotted two minutes, and at some point, she heard the door open.

She didn't realise she'd been crying until he said something, a curse, and crossed to the edge of the bed, sitting down on it heavily and moving his hand to her cheek, gently wiping away the moisture there. His expression was grim, his eyes impossible to read, but his fingertips were soft and determined, moving to remove the physical signs of her emotions.

'I would do anything in the world not to have had to do this,' he finally said, the words dragged from him.

She knew that to be the truth. This marriage wasn't what he wanted either. He was as trapped by their baby as she was. 'I know that.' She pushed up to sitting, dislodging his touch, lifting her own hands to wipe at the rest of her cheeks.

'I'm fine.' She was glad her voice sounded clear. 'I've just been more prone to emotions since I got pregnant. It's out of my control.'

It didn't exonerate him. He continued to look at her as though he were fighting a battle with a superhuman force. He hated this. She was openly expressing her disbelief, he was holding his deep inside him, but there was no doubting that both of their lives had been torn open by this pregnancy.

'What did you want to talk about?'

His jaw clenched. 'Will you eat something?'

His words were so reminiscent of the version of him she'd known in New York that for a moment she let herself slip back through the cracks of time, cracks that yearning had opened wider. 'I'd kill for a coffee.'

'Murder is not necessary,' he responded immediately. 'Though I could understand if you felt a little driven to it.' A joke. A smile teased the corner of her lips but her mouth and heart were too heavy to oblige.

'Come.' He stood and her stomach rolled.

She nodded slowly. 'I'll just be a moment.'

He hesitated.

'I'm coming. Honestly.'

A crisp nod. 'Fine. This preparation is important, Daisy. It's for your sake, so you know what to expect.'

Anxiety shifted through her. 'Okay.'

In the bathroom—smaller than the main one she'd passed—she took a moment to freshen up, brushing her hair and teeth, washing her face and applying a little gloss to lips that felt dry courtesy of the aeroplane's air conditioning. But she worked quickly, aware that time was passing, bringing them closer to the RKH and her future as its queen.

He was in the main living space of the plane, but he wasn't alone. Six men and three women were sitting with him, each dressed in suits, so that in contrast Sariq in his robe looked impossibly regal and forbidding. When she entered, all eyes turned to her, yet she felt only the slow burn of Sariq's.

'Leave us.'

Their response was automatic. Everyone stood, moving past Daisy, pausing briefly to dip their heads in a bow that was deferential and unsettling. When she turned back to Sariq, he was standing, still watching her.

'Some members of my government,' he explained.

'Women?' She moved to the table, deliberately choosing a seat that was several away from him, preferring a little physical separation even though it did little to quell the butterflies that were rampaging through her system.

'This surprises you?'

'I guess so.'

'The RKH is not so out of step with the west. Women hold the same rights as men.'

A woman appeared then, carrying a tray, which she placed in front of Daisy. The aroma of coffee almost brought a fresh wave of tears to her eyes. It was so familiar, so comforting, that she smiled with genuine pleasure at the attendant.

'Thank you.'

'*Ha shalam.*' The attendant smiled back, encouragingly.

'*Ha shalam* means thank you,' Sariq explained. Daisy repeated it.

'This is Zahrah. She will be your primary aide.'

'I am pleased to meet you, Your Highness.'

Zahrah bowed as the others had, but lower, and she lifted Daisy's hand in her own, squeezing it. Her eyes were kind, her smile gentle and friendly. The woman was beautiful, with glossy dark hair, long, elegant fingers, and nails painted a matte black. Daisy's heart swelled. Something like relief flooded her.

'She will help you ease into this,' Sariq continued. 'To learn the language and customs of my people, coordinate your schedule, oversee your needs.'

'I think I'll need a lot of help,' Daisy murmured, lifting her brows, the words directed towards Zahrah.

'You're too modest, Your Highness.'

'Please, call me Daisy,' she insisted.

In response, Zahrah smiled and bowed once more before leaving the cabin.

'She won't do that.'

It took Daisy a moment to understand what he meant.

'Do you remember in New York, how hard you found it to use my name?'

Daisy sipped her coffee without answering.

'And you are a foreigner with very little understanding of royalty and its power. Imagine having been raised to serve the royal family, as Zahrah was. Deference is ingrained in her. Do not let it unsettle you. Being treated like this is something you will have to become accustomed to.'

'I don't know if I can—I'm just a normal person. I can't imagine being treated as anything other than that.'

'In the RKH, you are equal to only one person. Me. To everyone else, you are like a goddess.'

A shiver ran down her spine. 'And this is how you were raised? To see yourself as a god?'

'I don't see myself that way.' His response was swift and there was a heaviness to the words. 'Gods have unlimited power. I do not.'

'I'm glad you realise that.' The words were delivered drily but a smile flicked across his lips, widening the cracks into the past. She gripped onto the present with both hands, refusing to let herself remember what that weekend had been like. It was a lifetime ago, and they were two different people. Then, they'd been together by choice. Now? Circumstances required it, that was all.

'When we land, there will be a small group of photographers, vetted by the palace. You will step out of the aircraft first, onto a platform, where you will stand alone a moment and wave. It will be morning in Haleth, and not too warm yet. I will join you once they have had a moment to take a photograph of you alone. Protocol dictates that we do not touch, publicly.'

She lifted a brow. 'That seems somewhat arcane, given I'm pregnant with your baby.'

'It is as it is.' He lifted his shoulders.

'Fine by me.' She sipped her coffee, closing her eyes for a moment as the flavour reached inside her, comforting her, bringing peace to her fractured soul. 'I'd prefer it that way, anyway.'

His eyes flashed with something she couldn't interpret. Mockery? Frustration? Pain? She blinked away.

'You are afraid.'

'Of you? No.'

'Not of me.' He didn't move, but his words seemed to wrap around her. 'Of yourself.'

'What?' She took a gulp of coffee.

'You are afraid of wanting me, even after what's just happened.'

Her heart began to thud inside her. She couldn't tear her eyes away from him, and there was a silent plea on her features, a look of confusion and uncertainty, and, yes, of want. Of need.

He stood then, bringing himself to the space beside her, propping his bottom on the edge of the table and spinning her chair, so she was facing him. 'We should not have slept together.' His hand lifted to her hair, running over its find gold ends as though he couldn't help himself. 'I knew I wanted you the moment I saw you, and yet you should have been off-limits to me.'

His hand dropped to her cheek. 'Just as I should have been to you. And yet we couldn't stop this.'

She swallowed, her throat shifting with the movement. His hand dropped to her shoulder, his thumb padding across the exposed bone there. 'I want to promise you I won't touch you again, but I am afraid too, Daisy.'

The admission surprised her.

'I am terrified of how much I want you, even now. Even when I know you must hate me for bringing you here, for railroading you into this marriage.'

Her mouth was so dry. She could only stare up at him, but his confession was tangling her into a thousand knots.

'I do hate what you did,' was all she could say.

His eyes swept shut, briefly, his lashes thick and dark against his caramel skin. Her stomach hurt. Her heart ached. Her body was alive with fire and flames and yet inside there was a kernel of ice that refused to budge.

'I can conquer this,' he said simply, dropping his hand and standing. 'I had no choice but to marry you, but I will not sleep with you again. You have my word.' His hand formed a fist at his side as though even then he was having to force himself to rail against his instincts and not touch her. 'You do not need to fear this.'

Oh, but she did. She was terrified of how she

wanted him. Hearing him be so honest about his own struggles made her acknowledge her own—inwardly at least. Yes, she wanted him. Even as they'd said their vows her insides had been heating up, her body acknowledging that, in him, she had met her perfect match.

But she could barely admit that to herself, let alone to him. 'Thank you. I appreciate that.'

So prim! So formal! Good. Let him think she was grateful for this reprieve instead of desperately wanting to contradict his edict.

If he was disappointed, he didn't show it. 'Let's keep going. There is much you need to know before we land.'

# CHAPTER NINE

IN NEW YORK, he'd made a promise to her. Space. Time. Freedom to think, away from him. And he intended to uphold it even when the knowledge that she was in the palace, only a wall separating them, had him wanting to go to her, to speak to her, to see her, to assure himself she was okay. Yet he had made this promise and it seemed small, in the scheme of all that he was asking of her, and therefore vital that he respect it.

In the three weeks since they'd arrived in the RKH, he'd upheld his promise. Maintaining his distance, receiving his updates from Zahrah to assure himself that Daisy was coping, and that she was well. He'd organised medical appointments to ascertain her physical health, and that of the baby. And he'd managed the politics of their marriage like a bull at a gate. A top PR firm was engaged to sell the message in the media. This was a new age for the country and his marriage to Daisy Carrington symbolised a step forward with the west. Reaction had been, for the most part, positive. Though there were some quarters that publicly questioned his choice and voiced great offence that the Sheikh of the RKH should turn his nose up at the two women who had widely been known to be candidates as his prospective Emira.

As for those women, he'd met with each privately, and to them he'd sold it as a love story.

*'I was not prepared for how I would feel to meet her. I wish I had been able to resist, but there were greater forces at play.'*

It had been easy to sell that message. It hadn't been love at first sight with Daisy, but it had been infatuation, and that was equally blinding.

There were those who seemed to accept his choice to marry an American, but not Daisy. Stories about her had run in the press. Fewer in the RKH papers, which were generally respectful of the palace and its privacy, but, in the blogs and cheaper tabloids, derisive pieces about her status as a divorced woman had been printed. Someone had found photos of her first wedding, so he'd seen her smiling up at her first husband, and something inside him had fired to life, filling him with darkness and questions. He wanted to know about this man she'd married—by choice. The man she must have loved at some point, even if she didn't now.

And he'd wanted to silence the stories that speculated on all sorts of things in Daisy's life before him, things he knew to be false without having had the conversations. Rumours that she'd travelled across America with a rock band, the inference being that she'd slept with the whole slew of musicians. Suggestions that her role at the hotel had been to appease guests in whatever manner she found suitable. And yes, the inevitable suggestion that this baby wasn't actually his.

He had read them with fury at first and, as the weeks went by, with muted anger and disbelief and, finally, with guilt and regret. She didn't deserve this.

'Has she read them?' he'd asked Zahrah on the fifth morning.

'I believe so, Your Highness.'

A grim line had lodged on his lips and it hadn't lifted since, and after three weeks of feeling as if he wanted to see her, to ensure she was okay, but resisting that impulse because she'd asked it of him, he was close to the breaking point.

So it wasn't precisely Malik's fault that they argued. Sariq had been ready to unleash his fury at anyone who looked at him the wrong way, let alone what Malik said.

'You cannot blame these people, sir. She is not suitable and it will take time for the country to adjust their expectations.'

Fire had filled Sariq's blood. 'In what way is your Emira not suitable?'

Malik hadn't appeared to realise he was on dangerous ground. 'Her nationality. Her marital status. Her pedigree.'

'If I have no issue with these things, how dare you?'

Malik's head jerked back. 'I beg your pardon, sir, I did not mean to offend you. I have spent my life protecting your interests...'

'My interests are now her interests.'

Malik was silent.

'You will organise a ball. Invite the parliament and foreign diplomats. It's time for the people of Haleth to meet my wife.'

Malik dipped his head but it showed scepticism.

'She is pregnant with my child.' Malik scraped his chair back and moved towards the open doors that led to the balcony. A light breeze was lifting off the desert, bringing with it the fragrance of sand and ash, and a hint of relief from the day's warmth. 'I wish, more than anything, that it hadn't been necessary to marry her.' His shoulders were squared as he remembered the way he'd had to bully Daisy into this. Regret perforated his being. 'She is now my wife. That's all there is to it.'

It was another baking-hot day. Daisy stood where she was, on the balcony that wrapped around this segment of the palace, staring out at the shimmering blue sky and desert sands that seemed to glow in the midday sun until a raised voice caught her attention. She turned in that direction right as a door pushed open and Sariq strode out, his frame magnetic to her gaze, his expression like thunder.

She stayed right where she was, frozen to the spot, her eyes feasting on him, her brain telling her to move, her blood insisting that she stay. It had been three weeks since she'd seen him. True to his word, he'd left her in peace, and she knew she should have been gratified that he'd respected her wishes, but deep down she felt so lonely, and so afraid.

Emotions she'd never show him, though. She tilted her chin in defiance. At least he looked as surprised to see her as she felt to see him. His chest moved with the force of his breathing; it was clear he was in a bad temper.

But why?

The raised voices—had one belonged to him?

Her mouth felt dry, and that had nothing to do with the arid desert climate.

He stared at her as though he was trying to frame words and she stared back until the silence became unbearable. What did she have to say to this man, anyway?

His eyes roamed her face in a way that sparked fires in her blood. How she resented his easy ability to do that! She felt her nipples pucker against the lace of her bra and her abdomen clenched hard with unmistakable lust. A biological response that she had no intention of obeying.

A bird flapped overhead, its wingspan enormous, drawing Daisy's gaze. She watched as it circled the desert and then began to drift downwards, its descent controlled and elegant.

It flew beyond her sight and so she looked away, back to Sariq. He was frowning now, but still regarding her with the full force of his attention, as though he could understand her if only he looked for long enough. But she didn't want to be understood.

Swallowing to bring much-needed moisture back to her mouth, she said quietly, 'Excuse me,' before turning and heading into the blessed cool of the tiled sitting room of the palace. Her heart though wouldn't stop hammering. She knew their suites of rooms were in close proximity, but she hadn't realised this balcony was shared by both. It seemed to create a greater intimacy than she was comfortable with. She used this space often, particularly in the evenings when the sting of the day's heat had dropped, and she was able to sit beneath the blanket of jewels dotted through the inky night sky, reading or simply existing, quiet and contemplative.

'Daisy.' His voice held a command. She ignored it. 'Daisy.'

Damn it. He was closer now, his voice right behind her. She stopped walking and turned, but she was unprepared for this—the full force of attraction that would assail her at his proximity. But attraction was beside the point—she wouldn't give in to that again.

'Yes, sir?'

He closed his eyes, his nostrils flaring as he inhaled. 'Sariq.'

'Yes, Sariq?'

He latched his gaze to hers and her pulse throbbed through her. Still, he stared, and for so long that she wondered if he had any intention of speaking. She was about to turn away from him anew when his gaze dropped to her stomach and a hint of guilt peppered her mood. She was pregnant with his child, and he'd spent three weeks away from her. Naturally he was curious.

'I'm fine. The baby's fine, too. We had a scan two weeks ago.'

'I know.'

'You do?'

And then, a smile lifted one corner of his lips, a grudging smile that wasn't exactly born of happiness. 'Did you think I wouldn't involve myself in the medical care of our child?'

Their child. This had nothing to do with her.

'How are you?'

'This wasn't included in your report?'

'Basic health information.' He shrugged with ingrained arrogance. 'Nothing more.'

'What more is there of consequence?'

His brows knitted together. Her tone was unmistakably caustic. 'You're happy?'

She couldn't help the sceptical laugh that burst from her. 'Really?'

'Zahrah says you're settling into your routine well?'

Daisy ignored the prickle of betrayal that shifted inside her. Everyone in this palace reported to Sariq. It shouldn't surprise her that the servant she'd begun to think of as a friend was doing likewise. 'My routine involves being pampered around the clock. I don't imagine many people would struggle with that.'

Frustration, though, weaved through her words. 'But you do,' he insisted. 'You don't like it.'

Her expression was a grimace. 'I'm more comfortable doing the pampering than I am being spoiled. I don't need all this.' She lifted a hand to her head, where her blonde hair had been braided and styled into an elaborate up-do. 'I'm not used to it.'

'You'll become used to it.'

A mutinous expression crossed her face. 'Do I have to?'

'Yes.' And then, more softly, 'You're aware of the media stories?'

Pain sliced inside her being. She wrenched her face away, unable to meet his eyes. Some of the stories—most, in fact—had been absolutely appalling. 'Are you wondering how many are true?'

He said a word in his own language that, going by the tone and inflection, was a bitter curse. 'I am asking how these preposterous stories have affected you. This has nothing to do with me.'

'You don't care that I'm a rock star groupie?'

'I don't care about any of it.' But something in his eyes showed that to be a lie. He wasn't being completely honest to her, and she hated that. She hated that he might have read the headlines and believed them, that he might believe she'd made a habit of sleeping with guests of the hotel. After everything she'd been through with Max, Daisy had made a point of remaining guarded with members of the opposite sex.

The irony of these stories—when she'd been a virgin on her wedding night, and slept with no one since her divorce—filled her with a desire to defend herself. Except Sariq didn't deserve that. What did it matter if he thought her promiscuous? Who cared? As if he hadn't had his share of lovers in the past?

There was only one element of the stories that she cared to contradict. 'You are the father.'

A look of anger slashed his features. 'I know this.'

She bit down on her lip then, staring out at the desert. 'We were together two nights, but it was enough for me to see inside your soul, Daisy Al Antarah.' It was the first time her new name had been spoken aloud to her and it sent a *frisson* of response shuttling down her spine. 'I saw you and I wanted you. I seduced you. There was nothing practised about your responses to me. I am aware that I put you in the position of doing something outside your usual comfort zone.'

Which meant what? That she was bad in bed? Great. It was a silly thing to care about in that moment. A thought not worthy of her, so she relegated it to the back of her mind.

'I should have seen the signs. Perhaps I did, and chose to ignore them.'

'What signs?'

'Your inexperience, your innocence.' He shook his head, as though he were angry at himself. 'I knew you were out of your depth and I ignored that because it suited me, because I wanted you, and now we must both pay the price for that.'

Something like pain clenched her heart, because his regret was heavy in the tone of his words, but, more than that, she could feel it emanating off his frame. 'You don't want me here.'

He shifted his gaze to hers without speaking.

'You wish this hadn't happened, that we weren't married.'

A muscle jerked in his jaw and he regarded her silently. When the air between them was unbearably thick with tension, Daisy took a small step backwards, intending to leave, but his hand on hers stilled her.

She froze, her body screaming at her for something she couldn't fathom. 'Don't *you* wish that, Daisy?'

Wish what? She swept her eyes shut for a moment, gathering thoughts that had been scattered by his simple touch. As she stood there, his thumb began to move slowly over her inner wrist, sending pins and needles scuttling through her veins.

'I…' She darted her tongue out to moisten

her lower lip at the same moment she opened her eyes, so she saw the way his attention was drawn to her mouth and the flame of desire began to spark harder.

'This marriage is the last thing either of us wanted.' The words were soft, and yet they cut something deep inside her. 'When we met in New York, I was in a deep state of grief.' Her heart softened. 'I was weak, where you were concerned. I wanted someone to take the pain of loss away, and you did. When you came to my bed, it obliterated everything besides my need for you.'

She stared up at him, her heart thudding in her chest. Her head and her emotions were at war with one another. Everything she knew she felt about men and love and sex demanded that she pull away from him, but instincts and feelings were holding her right where she was, a flash of sympathy making her want to comfort him and reassure him even when she doubted he deserved that.

'I wanted to be with you,' she said quietly, absolving him of the guilt of feeling that he'd overruled her in some way. 'Believe me, if I hadn't, I would have been perfectly capable of shutting down your advances.'

He lifted his other hand, reaching it around

behind her head to the pins that kept her style in place. 'You had to do so many times, I suppose.'

Pain shifted inside her. 'The articles aren't true.'

'We've covered that.' Each pin he removed, he dropped to the ground, so there was a quiet tinkling sound before he moved on to the next. 'That doesn't mean you weren't the object of interest from many guests before me.'

A hint of heat coloured her cheeks, because he was right. 'From time to time. But I've always found it easy to deflect unwanted attention.'

'To fade into the background,' he remembered, moving to the fourth pin, loosening it so a braid began to fall from her crown.

'As my job required of me.' Why did her voice sound so husky, so coarse?

'And you tried to do this with me.' Another pin dropped.

It shouldn't have been biologically possible, but somehow Daisy's heart had moved position, taking up real estate in the column of her throat. 'Not hard enough.'

His eyes narrowed by the smallest amount. Another pin dropped. And another. When he spoke, he was so close his breath warmed her temple. One braid fell completely. His gaze moved to the side as his fingers worked at freeing it completely, so half her hair hung loose about her face. 'Do you think you could have done anything that would have put a stop to what we shared?'

It was hard to speak with her heart in her throat. 'Are you saying you wouldn't have taken "no" for an answer?'

The other braid fell. 'I'm saying you weren't capable of resisting what was happening between us.'

She wanted to defy him, to deny that fiercely, but there was a part of her that knew he spoke the truth. 'You're wrong.' The words were feeble.

He ignored them. 'So step away from me now.' He loosened the braid. She held her breath, staring up at him, fierce needs locking her to the spot when her brain was shouting at her to draw back, to show him that he was wrong about her, that she was very much in control of her responses to him.

But she wasn't and never had been, and she hated that.

Challenge lay between them, sharp like a blade. The air was thick and nothing could ease it. Breathing hurt.

'I told you I wouldn't touch you.' His fingers loosened her hair. A breeze lifted it so some ran across her cheek. 'I intend to honour that promise until you release me from it.'

Her harsh intake of breath sounded between them. That wasn't fair. She couldn't want him—

she sure as heck shouldn't—but her knees were trembling and heat was building between her thighs, whispering promises she desperately wanted to obey.

'Sariq.' She didn't know what she wanted to say, but his name seemed like a good place holder, and she liked the way it felt on her lips, as though it were a promise. But of what?

'If I kissed you…' he moved his hand to her lips, padding his thumb over her flesh '…we'd be in bed within minutes. If we even made it that far.'

Her temperature spiked at the vivid imagery.

'Just like in New York.'

Her lips parted.

'You see, your body tells me a story, *habibte*. I see desire in your eyes, with how wide they flare and how dark your pupils are. Your cheeks are pink, your breathing rushed as though you have run a marathon. Your breasts move quickly as you try to fill your lungs, and your nipples…' he dropped his gaze '…have been begging for my attention since I stopped you from leaving this room. If I touched your most intimate places, I would feel your heat and need for me against my palm, just as I did in New York.'

She sucked in a ragged breath.

'It would be easy for me to kiss you and make you forget the path you've chosen, just as I did in America. It would be easy for me to override your instincts and make you mine. But you would hate me for that, wouldn't you?'

Would she? She couldn't say. She was a mess.

'You think forcing me to marry you isn't already sufficient grounds for hate?'

The anger of her statement surprised her, though it shouldn't. She felt backed into a corner—lashing out was a normal response.

'It's ample,' he agreed with a small shift of his head, but his eyes were dark and they bore into hers.

'Why are you doing this?' she whispered quietly. 'You don't want this to be a real marriage. You told me that at the embassy that night.'

He pulled a face. 'I wasn't referring to sex.'

'No?'

His features shifted for a moment. 'I have known, all my life, that I would never love whomever I married. That's what I was referring to that night. So far as I'm concerned, sex is just a biological act. It can be shared without any true danger of intimacy.'

She felt as though her chest were being cleaved in two. She stared up at him, unable to explain the pain that was lashing her, or its source. But on some level, she found his assertion to be repugnant.

'And intimacy is bad?'

'It's not bad. It's simply not part of the equation for me. I accepted a long time ago that my duty to my country would require me to choose this path.'

He brought his body closer, so his broad chest was pressed to her breasts, and her nipples tingled painfully in anticipation. 'But sex? Sex without emotion, without love, can still be amazing.' He lifted a hand to her face, holding her still, and she caught her breath, waiting for him to kiss her, certain he would.

She felt his needs as surely as she did her own, his desire palpable, his body hardening against hers. Nothing moved, even the very air of the desert stood still, waiting, expectant.

'However, I swore I would keep my distance.' He dropped his hand and, with obvious regret, moved away from her. 'And I intend to honour that promise.'

It took several moments for her breathing to achieve anything close to normal.

'I have given you space, since you came to Haleth.'

Still, she couldn't speak.

'But three weeks without a sighting of the new Queen has left a hole for the media to fill. It's time for my people to begin a relationship with you.'

Her heart began to speed for a different reason now and anxiety caused a fine bead of perspiration to break out on her forehead. It took her several moments to remember how to form words. 'Do you mean…like an interview or something?'

'An interview is a good idea.' He nodded, no sign of the conversation they'd just had, which had left her all kinds of shaken up, in his handsome face. 'But initially, there is to be a ball. My parliament and foreign diplomats will attend. The event will be held in your honour.'

Whatever she'd been feeling moments ago was gone completely. 'Is that necessary?'

'Do you intend to stay hidden here for ever?'

She considered that. Did she? These last three weeks had been blessedly quiet but she'd been cognisant of the fact she was dodging her responsibilities, hiding from the world she knew to be out there.

'Do you care? About the rumours?'

He frowned. 'No.'

'So why does it matter?'

'Rumours in foreign papers that speculate on matters I know to be false? This is laughable. But you are the Emira of the RKH and my people must respect you; they must accept our child as their future ruler.'

A prickle of danger shifted through her.

'You're worried they might not? That this baby might not be accepted as your heir?'

'I'm not worried.' Nor did he look it. 'But I do not wish your life, or his, to be harder because of steps we could easily take now to smooth the way of this transition.'

It all made so much sense. She knew she should agree, but agreeing with Sariq stuck in her craw, so she maintained a somewhat dubious silence.

'Malik is organising the ball. I'll have Zahrah notify you of the details in due course.'

He couldn't sleep. Hours after he'd last seen Daisy, and he felt a curdling sense of foreboding, a kernel of worry he couldn't dispel. Telling himself he was being melodramatic, he threw his sheet back and stood, pacing to the small timber piece of furniture against the wall, lifting the ancient pewter jug and pouring himself a glass of water. In the distance, through the open doors of his bedroom, he could hear the familiar call of the *nuusha* bird, the night creature's song a cross between a bell and a whip. It was delicate and resounding, reaching across the desert from their nesting grounds in the cliffs of sand to the west of the palace.

He'd promised her he wouldn't touch her, but, oh, how he'd ached to do exactly that. When he'd seen her that afternoon, her cheeks pink from the heat, her hair so beautifully intricate but in a way he'd needed to loosen, so that he could remember the way it had fallen around her face when they'd made love…

He shouldn't think about that. He couldn't. Those nights were from a different lifetime, when he was free to act on impulse and she to indulge her desire.

He'd promised he wouldn't touch her and yet he'd come so close that day. He'd ached to kiss her. He very nearly had. And now, memories of her kept him awake, tormenting him, so he had a keening sense to go for a run, or a ride, to leave this gilded cage of a palace, to throw off the expectations incumbent upon him and be his own man. For one night. He strode onto the balcony, his eyes finding the looming shape of the caves, tracing their outline, wondering if he could absent himself from the palace for the four days it would take to make the round trip. There was an oasis there; he'd camped at its edges often.

Her strangled sound of surprise was barely audible at first, swallowed by the gentle breeze and the bird's cries.

It was as though he'd thought of her so hard and so often that she'd miraculously appeared before him. She wore a simple cream shift, barely covering her beautiful body, so he strained to keep his eyes on her face rather than allowing them to dip to the swell of cleavage revealed there. After their contact that day, seeing her like this was the last thing he needed. Knowing he had to be strong didn't alter the fact he wanted, more than anything, to drag her against him and make love to her.

'I…' Her tongue darted out, moistening her lips, just as it had earlier that day. His cock hardened.

'You couldn't sleep,' he murmured, knowing he should stay where he was, even when other forces were pushing him forwards, closing the distance between them.

She shook her head. Her hair was loose now, just as he'd wished it to be, and the breeze caught at the lengths, lifting them so a skein of the moon's light cut through it. Silver against gold. Magic and captivating.

When he'd read the articles, only one had caught his attention, only one had played on his mind as being worthy of examination. 'Tell me about your ex-husband.'

Even in the scarce light thrown by the full moon, he could make out the shift in her features, their arrangement into a mask of surprise, at first, and then hesitation.

'Max? Why do you want to know about him?'

'Did you love him?'

Her smile was cynical. 'I'm not like you, Sariq. Love is the only reason I would have ever married anyone.' And then, quickly, with a look of mortification, 'Present circumstances excluded, obviously.'

'Obviously.'

She turned away from him then, but her profile was all the more alluring for she was hiding herself from him. He had to move closer to see her better. He caught a hint of her delicate fragrance and his body tightened. His fingers ached to reach for her.

'And what happened to this great love, then?'

She angled her face to his, her clear eyes analytical, studying him in a way few had ever dared. It was unusual for Sariq to have an equal. Most people feared his power even when he wielded it so rarely, but Daisy was unflinching in his presence, and always had been.

'We got divorced. End of story.'

'I don't think so.'

'What do you want to know?' Her voice rang with discontent. 'All the gory details?'

'The pertinent ones at least.'

'Why?'

'You don't want to tell me?'

A flicker of a frown. He wanted to smudge his finger over her lips, but didn't. 'Is it relevant?'

'It's...of interest.'

She turned back to the view, her eyes following the sound of the bird in the distance. For a long time, she was quiet, and it was easy for Sariq to believe she had no intention of speaking. But then, finally, after a long exhalation, as if gearing herself up to discuss the matter: 'We met shortly after my mother died. I inherited. Not a lot—our house and her small investment portfolio. Enough for me not to have to worry about money for a while. It was her dearest wish that I pursue my musical career and I promised her—' Daisy paused, her voice becoming gravelled, her throat moving beneath his gaze as she swallowed fiercely so he felt a surprising urge to comfort her. 'I promised her I would. It was one of the last things I said to her.'

She was going to cry. He held himself rigid, adhering to his promise, but, oh, how that cost him when his arms were heavy with a need to drag her against him, to offer her physical comfort to her emotional wounds.

'After my father left, I stopped playing. I couldn't bear to any more. It was something we shared.' Her smile lacked warmth; it was a grimace of pain masquerading as something else, something brave when he could feel her pain. 'But then Mom got sick—' she frowned '—and it was one of the only things I could do to get through to her, to help her, so I played and I played and when she was well, she'd beg me never to give up. She'd beg me to play so everyone heard.'

Every answer spawned a new question. What had happened to her mother? Where had her father gone? They'd been so open and honest in New York, it had been easy to ask her whatever he wished, and he'd been confident she would answer. But there were barriers between them now, necessary and impenetrable, so he didn't ask. He stayed on topic even when a part of him wanted to digress.

'And your husband?'

'Max loved my playing too.' Her words were scrubbed raw. 'And I loved to play for him.'

Something moved in Sariq, and he wasn't naïve enough to pretend he didn't know what it was. Jealousy. He had listened to Daisy play and wished, on some level, that she were playing just for him.

'Max had a lot of big dreams. But they were… I helped him as much as I could. I trusted him implicitly. He was my husband, why wouldn't I? I wouldn't have married him if I hadn't.' Her eyes lifted to his and the strength of the ghosts there almost knocked the breath from his lungs.

'And?' His word held a command, there was that imperative he was used to employing, but it was born now not of regal title so much as a desperate hunger to comprehend. Something terrible had happened between them, he could feel it, and it was vital that he understand it.

'He lied to me.' The words were filled with bitterness. 'He didn't love me, he loved my inheritance and the implicit trust I had in him. Trust that led me to add him as a signatory to my accounts, that meant I never questioned his transactions. It wasn't until I began to prepare for the Juilliard that I realised he'd taken everything. *Everything.*'

Sariq was completely silent but inside, her explanation was exploding like the shattering of fine glass.

'Not only had he cleared my accounts, he'd taken out a mortgage on Mom's home, which I had owned clear of debt. I had to sell it, but that debt is still there, so I'm chipping away at it as best I can but...'

'It's onerous,' he supplied, after a moment, sympathy expressing itself in his tone.

'You could say that.' A bitter laugh. Then, her hand lifted to her throat, where a delicate line of diamonds ran across the detailing at the neckline of her nightgown. 'I suppose that's not one of my problems now.'

'Of course not.' Relief spread through him, because this was something real and palpable he could do, to relieve at least one of her worries. 'Have Zahrah provide Malik with the details and he shall clear this debt.'

'Have my people call your people?' she murmured, shifting to face him, so their bodies were only two or three inches apart.

'Something like that.'

Her features compressed with exasperation, and then her eyes lifted over his shoulder, so he wanted to reach out and drag her face to his, to look into her soul through their green depths. 'I thought I loved him, but, over the years, I've given it a lot of thought and, honestly, I think I was just so grateful.' The words were laced with self-directed anger.

'Why grateful?'

'When my dad left, it was easy to believe it had been my fault, that I was in some way unlovable. Then Mom died and I was all alone, and it was terrifying and empty and quiet. When Max appeared, he seemed to worship me. He was so full of praise and flattery and couldn't bear to be away from me.' She shook her head. 'It cooled once we were married. Now I see why: he got what he needed from me, but I was so grateful still, and I kept telling myself everything would be okay when my instincts were warning me all along.'

'Were you able to recoup any of the money?'

'He lost it.' She gripped the railing with one hand; the other remained at her side, as if weighted there by the burdensome diamond wedding ring he'd placed on her finger. 'Or hid it so well I didn't have the means to find it.'

'And so you took a job working at a hotel, trying to chip down a massive debt by waiting on demanding guests?'

'They weren't all demanding,' she corrected.

'If the debt is the size you're implying, surely that would have been a fool's errand?'

'What were my other options?' she pushed, a hint of steel touching the words. 'To accept defeat? To let him win?'

Her fierce fire stirred something to life in him.

'Many would have.'

'Not me.'

'No, not you.'

She swayed forward a little, but not enough. He remembered the way she'd felt that afternoon, her soft curves against his hard edges, and he wanted, more than anything, to feel that again. And then what?

The flicker of flames would convert to so much more. They would touch and he would kiss her, and then carry her to his bed where he'd spend the entire night reminding her that, aside from her pregnancy and their marriage, there was something between them that was all their own. But there couldn't be. All his life he'd understood the danger that came from caring for one's spouse. His father had been destroyed by his mother's death. Sariq would never care for anyone enough to feel their loss so keenly. His country deserved such sacrifice—his duty demanded that of him.

And perhaps she intuited the strengthening of his resolve, because she blinked, her huge eyes shifting to his with a look he couldn't comprehend, and then she stepped backwards, wrapping a single arm across her torso. 'It's late and I'm tired. Goodnight, Your Highness.'

She was gone before he could remind her to call him Sariq.

## CHAPTER TEN

HE READ THE intelligence report with a frown on his face that gave little of his anger away. But inside, a fury was unravelling that would know no bounds. 'And they were arrested at the border this morning?'

'Two security agents intercepted their vehicle as it crossed into the old town of Rika.'

'Armed?'

'To the teeth.'

Sariq's expression was grim. 'Where are they being held?'

'In the catacombs.'

'Fine.' He scraped his chair back. 'We shall go there now.'

Malik's displeasure was obvious. 'But, sir, the ball begins in an hour…'

'The ball will wait.' The words were louder—harsher—than he'd intended. With an effort, he brought his temper under control. 'These men were intending to kill my wife, were they not?'

'That is the charge, yes, Your Highness.'

'Then before I parade my wife in front of a slew of people, I would like to ascertain, beyond a shadow of a doubt, that they have no links to anyone in attendance this evening.'

'The guards will investigate this.'

Sariq held a hand up to silence his oldest, most loyal advisor. 'That is not sufficient. In this, I will not delegate.' He stalked towards the door. 'Come, Malik.'

Daisy wasn't sure what she'd expected. In the hotel in America, the ballroom was impossibly grand, with tall columns and exceptional art, but even that was nothing to this. A wing of the palace stood vacant of all furniture. The walls were gold, and each was decorated with an ancient piece of art. Flower arrangements were placed on marble pillars at regular intervals, so the air was rent with sweetness. At the end of the enormous room, glass doors had been thrown open to reveal a dance floor made of white marble tiles. While there were fairy lights strung across it, nothing dimmed the beauty of the desert night, the brightness of the stars that shone down on them. The music was traditional, lyre, flute and sitar combining to create an atmospheric and intriguing piece.

Daisy hovered above it all, waiting in the

wings, safe from being seen, her anxiety at the role she must play increasing with every moment that passed.

'He won't be much longer,' Zahrah, standing a little way away, murmured soothingly.

Daisy made an effort to relax her expression, even attempting a smile. 'It's fine.'

The music continued and, below her, beautifully dressed guests milled, champagne in some hands, iced tea in others. Some of the women wore western-style ball gowns with enormous diamonds and jewels at their throats. Others wore ornate gowns and robes, the delicate, bright scarves arranged over their hair, adding mystery and intrigue to their appearance.

Daisy had worn what Zahrah had provided her with. 'It was the Emira's,' Zahrah had explained.

'Who?'

'His Highness's mother.'

'Oh.' She'd dressed with a sense of reverence, careful not to break any of the delicate fabric that made up the ceremonial gown. White with gold, just as Sariq often wore, it was heavier than it looked courtesy of the yellow diamonds that were stitched into the neckline and waist. It glittered from every angle. At her throat, she wore a single yellow diamond, easily the size of a milk-bottle cap, and on top of her head, a tiara.

Her hands were covered by white satin gloves that came to her elbows. 'They're hot,' she'd murmured to Zahrah, when she'd pulled them on. 'Perhaps I'll give gloves a miss.'

'You must wear them. It's protocol.'

'Gloves?'

She'd made a noise of agreement. 'No one is allowed to touch your hand but the Sheikh.'

Daisy's brows had lifted.

'You're not serious?'

'It's tradition.'

'So I'm meant to wear gloves my whole life?'

'Well…' Zahrah had smiled kindly '… I think we can relax the traditions behind closed doors, just as much as you'd like to. But when on state business, it will be expected that you do this.'

Daisy had compressed her lips, biting back an observation about the silliness of such a requirement. Haleth was an ancient and proud country. There were many habits and rituals that were new to her, but that didn't mean she could stand in judgement of them.

The guests swirled beneath them, an array of fabulous colour and finery. Twenty minutes later, Daisy looked to Zahrah. 'This is becoming rude.'

Zahrah frowned. 'Madam?'

'Keeping all these people waiting. Where on earth is he?'

'The message I received just referred to urgent business, I'm sorry.'

'I hate the idea of going down there on my own, but surely that's preferable to ignoring the guests?'

Zahrah's alarm was obvious. 'You can't. Not for your first function. His Highness would never approve.'

Daisy's interest was piqued. 'Oh, wouldn't he?' The idea of flaunting his authority was wildly tempting and she couldn't really say why.

'Of what would I not approve?'

Daisy whirled around, her eyes catching those of her husband immediately. He wore another spectacular robe, this one emphasising the strength and virility of his frame, the darkness of his complexion. On the balcony, he was the man she'd met in New York, but like this, he was an untouchable ruler. There was something unusually forbidding in his appearance, a tightness in his frame that had her brows drawing together.

Zahrah bowed low at his entrance and before she could straighten, Sariq had dismissed her. 'Leave us. Allow no one to enter.'

'Yes, sir.'

Alone, Daisy gave her husband the full force of her attention. 'Where have you been? People have been here an hour. *I've* been here an hour.'

\* \* \*

He wasn't accustomed to being questioned by anyone, but somehow he'd become so used to that with Daisy that it no longer surprised him. He shouldn't have come here straight from the prison. It would have been far wiser to give his temper time to cool down, but the plans that he'd discovered on the would-be assassins had chilled him to the core. Seeing Daisy now, knowing he was the reason her life had potentially been in danger, filled him with a deep and immovable anger.

'An urgent matter called me away. Are you ready?' His voice was curt. He couldn't help it, though he knew he must. Daisy didn't deserve to feel the brunt of his anger. Even though the threat had been contained—his expert security teams had done just what they were supposed to and perceived a threat before it could come to the fore—the knowledge of what these men had planned sent a shiver down his spine.

'Sure.' Her smile was brave, but he detected her hesitation beneath it. Something pulled at his gut—guilt—a desire to absolve her from this life, to set her free from all of this. But even as he thought that, there was an answering certainty that he never would. That he couldn't. She was the mother of his child and her place was here with him. If this evening's arrests had taught him anything it was that her position as the mother to the heir of the RKH put her at grave risk. He intended to do what he could to protect her from that.

But at the doors that led to the wide, sweeping marble stairs that created the entrance to the room, she stopped. 'Wait.'

'What is it?'

When he angled his face to look at her, he saw that she was pale and alarm filled him. 'You're well?'

'I'm fine. I'm fine. I'm just...' She lifted a hand to her throat, pressing her gloved fingers to the enormous jewel there. 'You said they'd never accept me. A divorced American. Why do you think tonight will be any different?'

Her anxiety was palpable, and of his making. And yet, he'd been speaking the truth. 'You're my wife now. It *is* different.'

'But it's not. You were talking about why you couldn't marry me, about what was expected of you. No one wants me to be here with you.' She curved a hand over her stomach and his eyes dropped, following the gesture. Something moved inside him then because, without his notice, her stomach had become rounded. Not hugely, but enough. His child was growing inside her. Something locked into place within him, making words difficult to form for a moment.

'No one wants me to be pregnant with your child.'

The threat was contained. There was no danger to Daisy in this crowd. And yet he put a hand on her forearm and turned her to face him. 'Would you rather avoid tonight?'

Her eyes lifted to his, surprise in their depths, but it was squashed by defiance. 'No.' She looked towards the crowds once more. 'This ball has been organised in my honour, like you said. The least I can do is turn up, right?'

Admiration shifted through him. 'We won't stay long.'

Daisy was surprised when she realised she was enjoying herself. She wasn't sure what she'd expected. Hostility? Open dislike? And there had been some people who'd regarded her with obvious scepticism and misgiving, though she was shepherded away from those people by an attentive Sariq, who hadn't left her side all evening. For the most part, though, the crowd had been welcoming and generous. Most of the women she'd spoken to had conversed in English in deference to her. Sariq had translated for people who spoke only the native language.

Yes, she was enjoying herself but, after an hour of making small talk with strangers, her energy was flagging.

As if he could read her thoughts, Sariq leaned towards her, whispering in her ear so his warm breath filled her soul. 'There is a dance, and then we can leave.'

'A dance?' Of its own accord, her heart began to move faster, beating against her bones as though it were trying to rattle free.

'Just one.' His smile was alarming, because it reminded her so strongly of the way he'd been in New York. Seeing him like this surrounded by his people, she was in awe of not only his charisma, but also his strength and intellect. In every conversation, he was able to demonstrate a complete understanding of matters that affected his people. Whether it was irrigating agricultural areas to the north or challenges facing the country's education system, he was informed, nimble and considered. She listened to him and saw how easy it had been for him to work his way into her being.

It hadn't purely been a physical connection between them. While she found him attractive, it was so much more than that. And suddenly, out of nowhere, she was struck by a desire to be alone with Sariq, to have the full force of his attention on her as it had been in New York, and briefly on the balcony that evening several weeks ago.

'Ready?'

She bit down on her lip and nodded slowly, her heart slowing down to a gentle thud. 'Okay.'

'Don't look so afraid,' he murmured in her ear, so only she could hear. 'We have a deal, remember? This is just for show.'

Her heart turned over in her chest and she pulled back, so she could look in his eyes. Just for show.

This marriage was the last thing he wanted. She needed to remember that. While it was inevitable that they'd get to know one another, she'd be a fool to hope for more.

To hope for more?

Her insides squirmed. What was she thinking? She was the one who'd sworn off marriage. She'd promised herself she'd never again be stupid enough to get so caught up in a fantasy that she lost who she was. No one deserved that, least of all this man, who'd insinuated she was good enough to take to his bed as a mistress but not good enough to marry. The man who'd told her, point blank, that he'd never love his wife. That, for him, sex and intimacy were two separate considerations.

She straightened her spine, thrilled to have remembered such pertinent facts before his body enfolded hers, drawing her close to him. And as if by some silent cue, the music paused and another piece began to play, slow and lilting.

With the stars shining overhead, the dance floor cleared so it was only Sariq and Daisy, their bodies moving as if one.

'You dance well.'

She wasn't sure she could take the compliment. He led, she followed—it was effortless and easy. They matched one another's movements as though they'd been designed to do just that. But they were silent and, after a few moments, that began to pull at her nerves.

'This is such an incredible courtyard.' For now, from this vantage point, she could see that the dance floor was surrounded on three sides of the palace. On the fourth, the view opened up to a manicured garden in the foreground and, beyond it, the desert. The wildness of the outlook, juxtaposed with the grandeur of this ancient building, created a striking effect.

'It was one of the first parts of the palace. In the eleventh century, these walls were erected. This courtyard was, then, the court, where the Emir presided over official matters.'

'Really?'

He made a sound of agreement. 'Over there—' he gestured with his hand, so she followed the gesture '—you can see the relics of the throne.'

And indeed, she could. It was made of marble, only a leg remained, but it was cordoned

off, as though it were an object of great value.
'The walls provided defence—from enemies
and sandstorms that are rife in this region.'

She looked around the courtyard with renewed interest, making a mental note to come
back and study it in more detail in daylight.

'Where is your court now?'

'I have an office,' he responded with a smile
that was lightly teasing. Her belly flopped.
'Here, at the palace, and one in the city. There
are state rooms for conducting the *rukbar*.'

'What's the *rukbar*?' She repeated the for-
eign-sounding word, imitating his accent.

'Very good.'

His approval warmed her.

'Literally translated, it means "relief". It is
a day each month when the palace doors are
thrown open and anyone, regardless of their
wealth and stature, may come to the palace.'

'What for?'

'To eat and be seen.' His smile deepened,
and a kaleidoscope of butterflies launched itself through her belly. 'The tradition began in
my great-grandfather's day, when poverty and
famine were crippling in this country. The palace provided a banquet for any who could make
it, and, more than this, he sat in and listened to
people's needs from dawn until nightfall, helping where he could.'

Daisy had slowed down without realising it. Sariq shifted, moving her with him. 'You still do this?'

He dipped his head in silent agreement.

'How do you help people?'

'It varies. Sometimes it's a question of a child not being able to get into school, in which case Malik has the education secretary look into matters. Other times, it's a family where the father has died and the mother cannot work, in which case we grant a stipend to help support her.' He lifted his shoulders in a gesture of nonchalance but there was an expression in his face that robbed Daisy of breath. 'In Haleth, you would never have struggled as you have.'

Daisy's feet stopped obeying her altogether. She was moving purely under Sariq's guidance. 'No?'

'No.' He lifted a hand, brushing his fingertips across her cheek as though he couldn't help himself. 'Here in Haleth, you would have come to me and I would have had Max held for questioning before he could "lose" your money.'

'Just like that?'

'Just like that.'

Her smile was lopsided. 'So you're the knight in shining armour for every distressed person in Haleth?'

'It's not possible to help everyone. We have social security agencies in place but the *ruk-*

*bar* provides a catch-all. An additional layer for the people.' He paused. 'The RKH is a phenomenally wealthy country. Distributing wealth wisely is one of the purviews of my role, and I intend to see the resources of this country benefit the people of the land.'

She felt the strength of his convictions and understood. She knew what his position meant to him. Admiration shifted inside her, and it brought with it a dark sense of foreboding. She didn't want to admire him; she didn't want to like him. But dancing beneath the stars in the arms of the man she'd married, Daisy felt as though a spell were being cast, and there was no antidote to it.

Sariq didn't believe in fate. He didn't believe in destiny. But dancing with his wife in the ancient courtyard, beneath a blanket of stars, he knew one thing: there was perfection in how they fitted together. Not only in the physical sense, but, more than that, in the way they thought.

He liked speaking with her. He liked hearing her thoughts, her answers. She fascinated him and intrigued him, and it was easy to see how he could become addicted to that.

'I'd like to see it.'

He didn't follow.

'The *rukbar*.'

Hearing her use his ancient language was an aphrodisiac. He kept moving, careful not to display the effect she had on him, even as his body was stirring to the beat of an ancient drum.

'It convenes in one week. I will advise Malik you shall join me.'

'Really?'

Her happiness stitched something in his gut. He nodded once. 'But I should warn you, Daisy, it can be harrowing. Some of the people who attend have nothing. Their stories are distressing.'

Her lips twisted in a way that made him want to drop his head and capture them with his own. He might have, to hell with the complications of that, if they hadn't been surrounded by hundreds of dignitaries.

'I can cope.' There was steel in her words, and he wondered at the cause of it. There was so much about her he didn't know, and yet he felt that on some level he understood every cell of her being. That wasn't enough though. The gaps in his knowledge of her seemed insupportable all of a sudden. There was an urgency shifting through him.

'Has anyone told you about the *tawhaj* tower?'

She frowned. 'No?'

He moved his fingers by a matter of degrees, stroking them lightly over the flesh at her back.

He felt her body tremble in response. Desire kicked up a notch.

'No.' Her voice was soft, husky. 'What is it?'

'Look.' He stopped dancing so he could gesture behind her. She shifted her gaze, her neck swanlike as she followed the direction he'd indicated. 'Do you see it?' He couldn't stop looking at her. He had to get a hold of this. They were being watched and the seduction they were enjoying was palpable. Surely everyone would be aware of the heat that was moving between them.

'No?'

'There.' It was an excuse to move closer. His arm brushed her nipples as he pointed more clearly and he felt her response. It was imperative that he remove them from this environment. He no longer wished to be surrounded by a hoard of onlookers. He needed his wife all to himself.

'Oh! Yes, I think so?'

It was, indeed, difficult to make out the tower in the moonlight. The spindly structure, forged from marble and stone many hundreds of years ago, was slender and elegant.

'Would you like to see it?'

She shifted to face him just as the music slowed to a stop. Her eyes held his and it was as though a question was moving from him to her, silent and unspoken, but heard nonetheless. 'Yes, Sariq. I would.'

## CHAPTER ELEVEN

His hand in the small of her back was addictive. They didn't speak as they moved through the ancient corridors of this palace. Floors of marble, walls of stone, tapestries, flowers, gold, jewels. It all passed in a blur. All Daisy was conscious of was the man beside her. His nearness, his touch, his warmth, his strength. She could feel his breathing as though it were her own.

It took several minutes for the noise of the party to fade from earshot completely and then there was silence, save for the sound of their footfalls and the pervasive throb of anticipation.

'In the thirteenth century, Haleth was made up of three separate kingdoms. War was frequent and bloody. The tower was built, initially, as a lookout. It is the highest point of palace land, and has a vantage point that, on a clear day, extends to the sea. It gave the Emir's forces the ability to detect a likely skirmish from a great distance.' He guided her through a pair of enormous timber doors, each carefully carved with scenes she would like to come back and study, another time.

'It meant that most of the approaches to the palace took place during sandstorms, when visibility was poor.'

She shivered. 'Such violence.'

'Yes.' He looked down at her, something unreadable in his expression. There was a tightening to his features that spoke of words unsaid.

'What is it?'

'Nothing.' He shook his head, as if to clear the thought. 'Here.'

They approached another set of doors. These were gold, and guarded on either side by two members of the RKH military, dressed as the guards in the embassy had been.

Sariq spoke in his own language, a short command. Each bowed low and then the guard on the left pulled a ring of brass keys from his pocket, inserted one into the door. Both guards worked in unison to open them.

Inside, there was a marble staircase, but it wasn't possible to see more than the first two steps. One of the guards moved ahead, and when Daisy and Sariq followed, she saw that the guard was lighting heavy lamps attached to the walls. The staircase smelled of kerosene and damp.

On they went, each tread worn down in the centre by the thousands of steps that had come before theirs, until finally the air grew clear, the stars shone overhead, and they emerged into an open room right at the top of the tower.

The guard was lighting the lamps, giving the space a warm glow, but Daisy barely noticed. She was too busy taking in the details of this spectacular tower. The walls were open, just spindly supports every few metres, to create the impression of windows where there were none. Those same spindles rose like the branches of a tree towards the sky, curving inwards at great height, stopping well before they reached the centre so the roof was open, showcasing the night sky in a way that was breathtaking. The moon was full and it caught the pale marble in such a way that it seemed to shine against the inky black of the heavens.

'Wow.'

The guard was leaving. They were alone.

'These pillars are incredible.' She moved to one, running her hands over the carefully carved shapes. 'They must have been made by talented craftsmen.'

His expression was rueful. 'They were carved by prisoners. I used to come here a lot, as a child.' His features grew serious and, without any elaboration, she understood what he was alluding to.

'After your mother died?'

Surprise flashed in the depths of his dark eyes. 'Yes.'

She nodded slowly. 'Losing a parent at seven must have been incredibly difficult. Were you and she close?'

His jaw clenched, and he stared out from the tower, his body rigid, as though he weren't going to speak.

'She was my mother.'

Daisy considered this. 'That's not an answer.'

His gaze pivoted to hers. 'Isn't it?'

She traced her finger over a line in the marble, following the swirling texture contemplatively. 'I loved my mother, but we weren't close. That didn't stop it from hurting like anything when she died. I think a relationship with your parents can be complex.'

'Why were you not close?'

She was conscious that he was moving their conversation to her, and perhaps it was a technique for deflection, a way of moving the spotlight off him. She allowed that, with every intention of returning to her question in a moment.

'My mother was bipolar.' It was amazing how easy she found that coming from her lips, when for years she'd grappled with discussing the truth of her home life. 'When she was in a manic phase, she was the most incredible fun.' Daisy shook her head, her brow furrowed as she looked up at the stars across the night sky. The view from here showcased the incredible silver of the desert sands, filling her with a desire to lift her wings and fly across its wide expanse.

'But there were times when that wasn't the case?'

'Oh, yes. Many times. As a child, I didn't understand it. I mean, one day she'd be pulling me out of school so we could go to the movies, or feeding me ice cream for breakfast, and then the next she wouldn't get out of bed.' She shook her head. 'Our house was either scrubbed to within an inch of its life, the smell of bleach on every surface, or completely abandoned. Milk cartons left out, dishes not washed, floors filthy.'

Sariq didn't say anything, but she felt the purpose for his silence. He was drawing her out, letting her keep talking, and despite the fact she generally kept her past to herself, she found the words tumbling from her now.

'There were times—when she stayed on her medication—when things were okay. But not really, because the medication just seemed to hollow her out. I don't think she really persisted in finding a good doctor and getting the right prescription. She hated the feeling of being "stable". Without the lows, she couldn't have the highs.'

'And your father?' Sariq prompted after a moment.

Daisy felt her throat thickening, as it often did when she thought of that time in her life. 'Dad couldn't deal with it. He tried to get Mom help but she was beyond that. He left home when I was ten.'

'Without you?'

'He wanted to take me. I refused. I knew my mom wouldn't cope.' She frowned. 'I was so angry with him, Sariq. To leave her just because she was sick? He failed her, and he failed me.'

'He did.' The words held a scathing indictment that was somehow buoying.

'Towards the end, Mom's manic phases grew fewer, her depression deeper. She began to self-medicate. Marijuana at first, then alcohol. Lots of alcohol.' Daisy closed her eyes, trying to blot out the pain. 'She was drunk when she crashed her car. Thankfully without hurting anyone else.'

He was quiet beside her but she felt his closeness and his strength and both were the balms to a soul that would always carry heavy wounds of her past. Silence sat between them, but it was a pleasant silence, wrapping around her, filling her with warmth. She blinked up at him and even though their eyes locked, she didn't look away.

He was staring at her and she felt something pass from him to her. There was magic in this tower, a great, appreciable force that weaved between them.

'When my mother died...' he spoke, finally '...my father sent me away. Partly for my own protection, but mainly, because I reminded him of her. He couldn't bear to spend time with me.'

She frowned. 'I thought...'

'Yes?' He prompted, when her voice trailed off into nothing.

'I just, the way you speak about him, I presumed you thought the world of your father.'

'He was an exceptional ruler. I admired him greatly. I feel his absence every day.' Sariq's gaze moved, returning to the desert beyond them. 'He loved only one person, his whole life. My mother. When she died, he lost a part of himself with her and he learned a valuable lesson.'

'What lesson?'

'That love leads to hurt.'

'Not always.'

'Really?' He lifted one brow, his scepticism obvious. 'You can say this after your own experience? Your father? Your husband?'

She bit down on her lip, wondering at his perspective.

'Dance with me?'

She blinked, looking around them. 'Here?'

'Why not?'

She was about to point out the absence of music, but she didn't. Because her heart was creating a beat in her ears, and it was all she needed. Wordlessly, she nodded, so he brought his arms around her waist, shaping her body to his.

They moved without speaking for several moments, but his revelations were playing through her mind. 'I think,' she murmured softly, 'that you don't know your own heart.'

He didn't respond, but that didn't matter. Deep in her own thoughts, she continued. 'Losing someone you love hurts. Betrayal hurts. But I don't think knowing there's a risk of that inures you to caring for another person. You think your father didn't love you? That you didn't love him? I think that's biologically impossible.'

'Your father didn't love you,' he pointed out after a beat had passed.

'Well, my dad's a somewhat deficient human. And anyway, he did love me. He just loved himself more.' She shook her head. 'Your father pushed you away because he was scared of being hurt again—because he knew that he loved you so much hurt was inevitable, if anything were to happen to you.'

He stroked her back in such a way that made it hard to hold onto a single ribbon of thought.

'Being afraid doesn't mean an absence of affection.'

'You're a romantic.' His words were murmured across her hair, teasing and light, pulling at her.

Was she? Daisy had never considered this to be the case. 'I think I'm more realist than romantic.'

'Not going by what you've just said.'

'Love is a reality of the human condition. You can't deny it's within you. You can't close yourself off to it. You loved your father and he died. The night we met, you weren't simply mourning a leader. You were grieving for the loss of your dad—something that goes beyond position and title. He was your father—the man who gave you life.'

Sariq stilled for a moment and then began to move, his steps drawing her towards the middle of the marble floor. 'It's different.'

'How? Why?'

He expelled a sigh. 'A royal child isn't… I was his heir. Not only his son. My purpose was always the continuation of the family.'

'You make it sound as though you were property rather than a person.'

'I was required.'

Daisy considered that a moment. 'Just like our child is "required"?'

A slight pause. 'Yes.'

The confirmation knotted her stomach in a way that was unpleasant. 'And so you won't love our child?'

'You are fixated on the notion of love.' The words were said lightly but they did nothing to ease the seriousness of her thoughts.

'I didn't have a father in my life for very long. I don't want my child to know the pain of an absent parent.'

'I was the one who insisted we raise our child together, wasn't I?'

'No.' She stopped dancing and looked up at him, her eyes sparking with emotions she couldn't contain. 'You insisted that I move here so your child would be in the RKH. Your heir. There's a difference.'

'What do you want me to say?'

She bit down on her lip, unable to put that into words. 'I don't want you to keep our child at an emotional distance,' she said, after several moments had passed. But it wasn't all-encompassing. She felt so much more.

*I don't want* you *to keep me at an emotional distance.*

'I won't.' The assurance was swiftly given, but it did little to assuage her concerns.

'Because I'd rather take my chances in America, regardless of what you say, than expose our child to the kind of upbringing you've described.'

He froze, his body completely still, his arms locked around her waist. There was such contrast—the strength and warmth of him juxtaposed to the rigid cool of his stance. 'America is not an option.'

Something flashed inside her. Anger! And it was so welcome. In the swirling, raging emotions she felt, anger was one she could grasp. It made sense. She liked it.

'You don't get to command me.'

His nostrils flared as he stared down at her, his attempt to control his temper obvious. 'You're wrong.'

'No, I'm not. You told me I was coming to the RKH as your equal. Well—' she pushed her hands onto her hips, glaring right back at him '—if I want to go to America then there's nothing you can do about it.'

His laugh lacked humour.

'I'm serious.'

'As am I. Deadly serious.' He brought his

body closer to hers, but it seemed accidental, as though he were simply moving without conscious thought. 'Do you know why I was late this evening?'

She shook her head.

'I was in the catacombs that run beneath the city. They were converted to prison cells a few decades ago. Two men are detained there, right now, who were planning on hurting you, Daisy.'

She froze, his words slamming into her like bricks. Out of nowhere, she began to tremble. Her ears rang with a high-pitched squealing sound. 'You're making that up.' She wanted to reject it. It couldn't be true.

'I wish I were.'

The shaking wouldn't stop.

Sariq swore under his breath, then his big, masculine hands were cupping her face, holding her steady for his inspection. 'Here, I can protect you. My guards can protect you. And believe me, Daisy, nothing matters more to me than your safety.' Neither of them moved. 'You and our child will have the full force of my army at your disposal. You must remain in the RKH. Can you see that?'

She nodded quickly. Fear—not for herself so much as for the life of her unborn child—was instinctive and swift. 'But why?'

His lips were a grim slash in his face. 'Because of what you represent. Because of the stability our child will bring.'

'I… Why didn't you tell me?'

'I just did.'

'I mean sooner.'

'I dealt with it.'

A shiver ran down her spine. 'What does that mean?'

'These men will not harm you.'

Her eyes flashed with fear. 'What did you do?'

His laugh was gruff. 'Not what I wished, believe me. They will spend a long time in prison for this though.'

'So if the threat is gone…'

'There are always madmen, Daisy, with political agendas.'

'You can't protect me from everything for ever.'

'No.' A muscle jerked in his jaw. 'But I can try.'

She thought of his mother then, who was murdered by madmen such as those apprehended this evening. His mother who had been pregnant with another child, and whose death had caused the beginning of the end for Sariq's relationship with his father. And a part of Daisy wanted, more than anything, to console Sariq. It was a selfish need though, because she also needed consoling. She needed distracting. She wanted to feel alive and safe, and present in the moment.

Reaching to her face, she pulled his hands away, stepping back from him to give them a little space. Then, slowly, deliberately, she reached for the straps of the dress, guiding them down her arms slowly, her eyes on his the whole time.

'What are you doing?' There was an expression of panic on his features, as though he knew that if she started this, he wouldn't be able to stop it.

'What does it look like?'

His eyes closed for a moment, then pierced her with their intensity. 'Daisy…'

She shook her head then, and the desert breeze lifted some of her fair blonde hair, blowing it across her cheeks.

'I don't want to think right now. I don't want to think about plots to kill me, threats, nothing. I don't want to think about dangers and politics.' The dress dropped to the floor at her feet. She stepped out of it, mindful of the beautiful silk lingerie she wore, grateful Zahrah had presented her with the set that evening.

'I just want to feel.' She stood where she was, her eyes fixed to his, her lips parted a little. 'Will you make me feel, Your Highness?'

Invoking that formal title made his eyes flare

wider. He released a low, growling sound, then shook his head, but it was obvious he was holding on by a thread. 'You'll regret this.'

'Perhaps.' She lifted her shoulders. 'But that doesn't mean I don't want it to happen right now.'

He took a step towards her and her breath hissed from between her teeth, sharp and intense. 'You don't know what you're asking of me.'

She lifted a brow. 'Really? Do you need me to spell it out?'

He didn't react to her attempt at humour.

'Make love to me, Sariq. Please.'

He cursed every word he knew in all the languages he spoke, but nothing helped. His wife—his beautiful, pregnant, desirable wife—was asking him to sleep with her and, despite the promise he'd made on the plane, he felt his resolve weakening.

He wanted her every bit as much as always. There was no absolving himself of this desire even when he knew it was fraught with potential dangers. They were married, true, but not for any reason other than this child. Becoming lovers could complicate that.

He needed to be clear.

He was a man of honour, and he had no intention of misleading his wife. 'Just sex.' He lifted a finger to her lips, pressing there gently. 'And just tonight.'

Her eyes flared wide and he held his breath, needing her to agree to his terms. He couldn't confuse what they were with physical desire. It had no part in this.

'If you say so.' Her eyelids fluttered and then she was pushing towards him, so he caught her in his hands, holding her to his body as he dropped his mouth and did what he'd been craving since the moment she'd walked into his embassy.

He kissed her, hard, hungrily, and it was like coming home.

Her eyes were heavy, her body too. She was warm, safe. Cradled against Sariq's chest, his heart beating beneath her ear. Steps, marble, kerosene. A door. She nuzzled closer. Something warm was wrapped around her, a robe? His robe? She inhaled. Yes, it smelled of him. Another door, footsteps. She closed her eyes. His heartbeat was steady, loud.

Another door. Something soft was beneath her. She forced her eyes open and looked around. Her room. Sariq, beside her bed.

'Don't go.' She lifted a hand, holding it towards him. 'Please.'

\* \* \*

If he were a man of honour, he would leave her now. For hours they'd pleasured one another, his body answering the call of hers, instincts driving them together, making it impossible to remember anything except the sense of what they each craved from the other. But in a few short hours the sun would crest over the desert dunes and reality would intrude.

She didn't want this, and nor did he. It was an illusion. A snatch out of time.

Danger lay before him. If he joined her in bed, he'd fall asleep. They'd wake up together, facing a new day as lovers.

His eyes dropped to her belly, rounded with his child, and a paternalistic pride fired in his belly. He owed it to their child not to mess this up. Sleeping with Daisy tonight had been, undeniably, perfect but it was also problematic. He wanted her.

He wanted her in a way that was addictive, that could threaten his legendary self-control if he didn't take care.

'It's late.' The words were crisp and he saw her flinch in response. He was already ruining this. Just as he'd said in the tower, pain brought pleasure and pleasure brought pain. 'Go to sleep.'

He left before she could respond.

# CHAPTER TWELVE

HE BARELY SLEPT. Just as the sun lifted above the desert, he pushed the sheet from his body and strode, naked except for a pair of boxer shorts, onto the balcony. Frustration gnawed at his gut. Dissatisfaction too.

He shouldn't have left her without an explanation.

He'd panicked, but she'd deserved better.

Without intending to, he moved along the balcony, towards the doors that led to her apartment. If she was asleep, which she surely would be at this hour, he would leave her. And if she was awake?

He stood on the other side of the glass, looking in at his wife's room, wondering at the thundering inside his chest. The morning was perfect. Clear and cool, none of the day's stinging temperature apparent yet.

Daisy slept. She was so peaceful like this, so beautiful. Memories flashed through his mind.

New York. Her smile. Her laugh. The fascination he'd felt with her from the beginning.

Her face when he'd propositioned her to become his mistress.

The obvious shock. Despite the normality of such an arrangement, she'd been offended. Her fire when she'd thrown her pregnancy at him, with no idea what that revelation would mean.

And finally, her words on the night they'd married.

*'I'm marrying you because I have to—not because I want to—and I will never forgive you for this. Tonight I'm going to become your wife and I may appear to accept that, I may appear to accept you, but I will always hate you for this. I love our child, and, for him or her, I will try to make our marriage amicable, at least on the surface, but don't you ever doubt how I really feel.'*

She'd begged him to make love to her in the tower, the night before. Their physical connection was real and raw. There was no questioning that. But beyond it? She hated him. She despised him, as she had every reason to.

Did she still though? Even after time had passed and they'd grown…what? Closer? Did he really think that? Did he really *want* that?

His heart thumped.

Yes.

He wanted it, and yes, they had. He'd shared more of himself with Daisy in the short course of their marriage than he had any other soul in his entire life. He'd felt painfully lonely when they'd met and now?

He didn't want to examine it because the answer terrified him.

He would never allow himself to love her. No woman, ever, but especially not Daisy. There was far too much risk there. If he ever really let himself care for her, he suspected he'd lose himself completely. When he'd confronted the prisoners in the catacombs the night before, he'd wanted to kill them with his bare hands. The impulse had assailed him from nowhere but it had been strong and desperate. The idea of anyone hurting Daisy had been anathema to him.

He stood up straighter, his breathing forced.

For Daisy, he would give up his kingdom, his crown. Anything she asked of him. Revulsion flooded him, and a heavy sense of guilt. Being Sheikh of Haleth was his purpose in life. He had been born and raised for this, and desire for a woman wasn't anywhere close to a good enough reason to doubt his duty.

Except it wasn't just desire, a voice niggled inside him. There was a complexity of considerations here, but none of these could permit him to forget what he owed his country.

He cursed under his breath and spun away, stalking back into his own room and dressing quickly. What he needed was to think.

All his life, Sariq's life had followed a path, a plan, and now he was stepping into the unknown. It wouldn't work. He didn't want it. He needed a new plan, one that would work for him, Daisy, and their child.

He needed to think without the knowledge that Daisy was only a wall away.

'Have a horse prepared. I'm going to the desert.'

He would never love her.

Daisy lay on her back, one hand on her stomach, patting the rounded shape there, her eyes chasing the detailing in the ceiling. Her body bore the marks of his lovemaking but it was all a lie. Sex and intimacy were not connected for Sariq.

How many times and in how many ways had he said this? Even at the embassy, when she'd first arrived and he'd asked her to become his mistress.

Why had that hurt so badly?

Her stomach dropped, because an answer was beating through her, demanding her attention. In New York, she'd been drawn to him because she'd never known anyone like him. And at the embassy, she'd been furious with him, but also, she'd felt a thousand and one things—good things.

And now?

She closed her eyes and remembered all of their conversations, shared moments, desire, need, a tangle of wants, impulses that had been pushing her towards him even when she wanted to dislike him so, so badly.

But for him?

*Just sex. And just tonight.*

Nothing had changed. It was the same parameters he'd established in New York, the same parameters he'd tried to enforce when he'd asked her to come to the RKH as his mistress. And every time he'd reminded her of those limitations, it had twisted inside her, like a snake's writhing. Pain, discontent. Why?

'Oh, crap.' She sat up, her throat thick with emotion. 'No.' She'd thought she loved Max when she'd married him, but she hadn't. She'd had no idea what love felt like—until now. It wasn't something you decided to do. It was all-consuming, a firestorm that ravaged your body. It was lighting her up now, making her feel… feel everything.

She'd fallen in love with her husband and that might ordinarily have been considered a good thing but, for Daisy, she couldn't see any way to make this work. He didn't love her. He never would. That was his one proviso.

Her stomach looped fiercely. Her heart contracted.

And suddenly, this marriage, this palace, the prospect of raising a child with him, felt like cement weighting her down. Living here with him had been scary enough, when he'd insisted on this marriage. She'd thought her fear came from the unknown, the pressure of being the mother to the royal heir. But it was so much more than that now.

She'd fallen in love with him, and he could never know. She couldn't tell him. She wouldn't.

But how could she keep it secret? Flashes of their night together came back to her. It might have been sex for him but every touch, every moment, had been a connection, a moment of love. She communicated her feelings in everything she did.

How could he not know?

And then what? If he realised how she felt?

Mortification curled her toes. He would become the third man in her life she'd offered herself to, the third man she'd loved or purported to love, who'd found it easy to withhold those same feelings. After her father, she'd been wary with men, but Max had found a way under her defences. After Max, she'd been wary to the extreme, but Sariq… It wasn't even that he'd charmed her. He hadn't. He'd been himself but there was something in his manner that had made it impossible for Daisy to forget.

But the idea of having *this* love rejected was anathema to her. It would hurt too much. She knew how he felt—she didn't need him to spell it out to her. No good could come from having this conversation.

Maybe she could make him love her? Her heart began to stammer. But she was being a fantasist. You couldn't make anyone who wasn't so inclined fall in love with you—as her first marriage had taught her.

At no point had Sariq given her even the slightest reason to hope. This feeling was her fault. Her mistake.

She had to conquer it.

He rode for hours, until the heat of the day, so familiar against his back, was almost unbearable. He rode towards the caves, knowing he would not make it there on this occasion. Knowing even as he set out from the palace that cowering from this wasn't worthy of him. He was not a man to run from anything, and he wouldn't run from this.

Last night was a mistake.

He couldn't blur the lines of what he wanted

from Daisy. She was right to insist on boundaries being in place. With every fast-moving step of the steed beneath him, his certainty grew that their marriage would only succeed if he insisted on structure. Formality. He'd been mistaken to let his interest in Daisy as a woman cloud what he needed from her.

Before he met her, he'd been preparing to marry, and his wife, whomever he chose, would have simply been a ceremonial addition to his life. Someone with whom he would have perfunctory sex for the sake of continuing the family line and then leave to her own devices.

He'd had no intention of having his bride installed in the apartment beside his own. That had been for Daisy, because to have her in his palace but any further from him felt wrong. His first instinct—and it had been a failure.

She was beautiful and desirable but how he felt about her personal charms was irrelevant now she was pregnant with his child. He wouldn't make the same mistake his father did. He wouldn't let affection for a woman weaken him.

He rode on, his face a mask of resolve. With every day that passed, he would conquer this.

It was some time around three when Daisy began to feel the exhaustion from the early start. Zahrah had woken her for the *rukbar* before day's break, so she could dress in a special ceremonial robe and be prepared for the procedures of the day.

'You'll sit beside Sariq. You won't need to say anything, though people will no doubt be very excited to see you. Some might ask to touch your belly—it is considered extreme good fortune to do so to any pregnant woman here in Haleth. But you, carrying the royal heir, your stomach would be seen as very fortunate.'

Daisy had found it hard to smile since the morning after she'd slept with Sariq. Having not seen him since then, she found that smile had felt even heavier, but she lifted it now, turning to see Zahrah. 'You haven't asked to touch my stomach.'

'I presumed you wouldn't want me to.'

Daisy lifted her shoulders. 'It's just a tummy.'

Zahrah extended a hand, her fingertips shaking a little, and it was in that moment Daisy understood the momentousness of this child she was carrying. Any child was special and important, but their baby meant so much to the entire country. Sariq had said as much at the embassy in Manhattan but she *could see that for herself* now. For Zahrah and she had become friends, yet the enormity of touching Daisy's pregnant belly was obviously overwhelming for Zahrah.

The sky was still dark when Zahrah led her towards the ancient rooms that bordered the courtyard where they'd had the ball a few nights earlier. Her eyes found the spot where they'd danced and ghosts of his touch lifted goose bumps over her skin.

'Here,' Zahrah murmured. It was only as Daisy approached she saw Sariq locked in serious conversation with Malik. He turned towards her, so she had only a moment to still her heart and calm her features. It was the first time she'd seen him since he'd carried her back to her bed. Since she'd asked him to stay and he'd left.

*Just sex. Just tonight.*

He'd been true to his word.

'Your Highness.' Malik bowed low.

Sariq said nothing.

Uncertainty squeezed her gut. 'Good morning.'

At that, Sariq nodded, his eyes holding hers for a moment too long before he turned back to Malik and finished his conversation. Daisy felt as though she were on a roller coaster, hurtling over the highest point at great speed.

'I'll be fine,' she assured Zahrah. 'You should go back to bed.'

Zahrah's smile was so normal. Daisy wished it could tether her back to her real self, to the woman she'd been before she realised how she felt. 'I'll be to the side of the room,' Zahrah murmured. 'If there's anything you need, just turn to me and I will come.'

Daisy nodded, but having this kind of attention bestowed on her still felt unusual. 'You're so kind to me.'

Zahrah smiled. 'You're easy to be kind to.' And she reached down and squeezed Daisy's hand. 'You'll be good at this. Have courage.'

It was a relief that Daisy's nervousness could be attributed to the *rukbar* she was about to take part in and not the first sighting of her husband in days.

Sariq spoke in his native tongue, which she was getting very proficient at understanding, if not speaking. 'Leave us now.'

Zahrah and Malik both moved further along, towards the doors that would lead to the room.

Now, Sariq offered a tight smile that was more like a grimace. 'You remembered.'

It was a strange thing to say. She lifted her eyes to his and felt as though she'd been scorched. 'You're still happy for me to be a part of this?'

Something flashed in his eyes and her stomach dropped. He wasn't happy. She didn't know how she knew it but she did. Waves of uncertainty lashed at her sides. 'The people will be gratified by your attendance.' It was so insufficient. The people. Not him.

A noise sounded, like banging against a door. 'That's our signal. Ready?'

And so it began. Once they were seated at two enormous, elaborate thrones made of gold and black metal, she'd heard the din from the external doors of the palace. A sense of fear and awe filled her when the doors were thrown open, but there was no stampede. An orderly queue had formed, and she learned, when they'd taken a small break to eat lunch, that security screening had been implemented, for the first time in the *rukbar*'s history, on the other side of the doors. Because of her?

Undoubtedly.

She'd seen his determination to keep her safe. For a moment that lifted her spirits until she remembered that her value, at this point, had more to do with her child than it did her.

She couldn't dwell on her own fracturing heart though. Not when the room was filling with people who were, so obviously, doing it tough.

Sariq listened patiently to each who came before him, offering a brief summary of each situation to Daisy in English once they'd finished speaking. Each story was hard—some were almost impossible to bear. Parents who'd lost children touched her the deepest of all. There were no medical bills here, the state provided, but there were other concerns. The cost of the funeral, the legacy of caring for other children while too grief-stricken to return to work.

Daisy felt tears filling her eyes on a number of occasions but worked hard not to show how deeply affected she was by these tragedies.

As the afternoon progressed though, she grew tired, her heart heavy, her mind exploding. And through it all, Sariq continued, looking as fresh as he had that morning, his concentration unwavering. She turned towards Zahrah, who immediately appeared at her side.

'Do you need something, Your Highness?'

'Just a little water.'

'Of course.'

Sariq turned to her, from the other side, and Malik paused proceedings. 'Are you okay?'

It was such a ludicrous question that she almost laughed. Okay? Would she ever be okay again? Did she even deserve to lament such a question in the face of so much suffering? 'I'm fine.' A bright smile and then a nod. 'Just thirsty.'

His eyes roamed her face, his expression unconvinced. 'You're pale.'

'I'm American.'

His impatience was obvious. 'Paler than usual.'

'I'm fine.' She couldn't say why she sounded angry at him, because she wasn't. Her anger was all directed at herself and her own stupidity for falling in love with a man who was so completely determined to be unavailable. 'Let's keep going. It sounds like there are still a tonne of people to see.'

And there were. The line continued until the sun set. 'Traditionally, this is when the *rukbar* concludes. Food is served in the adjoining room. I usually join the guests for a short time. You do not have to.'

'Of course I will,' she insisted, despite the fact she was bone-weary. Pride wouldn't let her show it. 'But do you have to stop now? There are people out there who've waited all day.'

His eyes clung to hers and then he nodded. 'Ten more.'

As Malik turned to the crowd to announce what the Sheikh had decided, Sariq leaned closer. 'Those that were not seen today will be given tickets for the next *rukbar*, so they're seen first. And any that feel they cannot wait have an email address to use to have their matter dealt with more speedily.'

That appeased her. The whole day had been eye-opening and fascinating. She felt, sitting beside Sariq, as though she was truly getting to know the fabric of this country. There was no hostility towards her—a divorced American. In fact, it was quite the opposite. People had been unstintingly kind, curious, polite.

Another hour stretched and then the *rukbar* was declared closed. Daisy was a little woozy when she stood, swaying slightly so that those in the room gasped and Sariq shot out a hand to steady her.

'I'm fine,' she said through a tight smile. 'Just not used to sitting down for so long.' He didn't relinquish his touch though, and her skin burned at the contact, her body throbbed, that same fire ignited, stealing through her soul. He guided her down the steps, away from the thrones, towards doors that led to another room.

'You should go to your room.'

Her gaze shifted. 'Is that an order?'

She saw the way his jaw tightened, and felt the battle raging within him. 'It's a suggestion.'

'Then I politely decline.'

He didn't like that, it was obvious. It wasn't fair to be angry with him. He'd done nothing wrong, nothing whatsoever. All along he'd been honest with her. Loving him was her fault, her problem. And yet she did feel anger towards him, because it simply wasn't fair. How could her heart be full to bursting and his determinedly empty?

'Daisy—'

'Everyone's waiting,' she said through clenched teeth, shifting away from him a little, just enough to dislodge his hand from her waist. 'Let's do this.'

Daisy was charming and lovely. He watched as she spoke to the assembled guests, moving from group to group and using the native language. He hadn't realised how good she'd become. Her accent was excellent and while she paused from time to time to search for a word, she was able to cover more than the basics. He watched the effect she had on his people and a warm sense of pride lifted him.

She was a natural.

No one, regardless of their lineage or birth, would have been a better Emira than Daisy. He turned back to his own conversation, listening to the rainfall statistics for the last quarter, but always he was aware of her location in the room. From time to time he would hear her laugh, soft but imprinted on him in such a way that meant he could pick it out easily. Would he ever lose this fascination with her? Would he have the ability to inhabit the same space and *not* hone in on her with every cell in his body?

Yes.

Of course.

Because that was what he wanted, and Sariq

knew that with determination and focus he could do anything he wished. Daisy was beneath his skin at the moment, but he would dispense with that in time. Once the baby was born, he could even contemplate giving her exactly what she wanted, sending her to live away from him.

His body tightened. Rejection, anger, dismissal. Doubt. Disgust. She wasn't a piece of trash he could simply discard once she'd served her purpose. And yet she was the one who'd suggested going to America.

But her security was of paramount concern. The men held in the prison beneath the city were not part of a wider organisation. They were rogue militants with their own agenda. There was no reason to think she was in any greater risk than she had been before, and yet the idea of any harm befalling her, even the slightest harm, filled him with the sense of burning acid.

His eyes found her once more. She was in conversation but she looked as though she wasn't listening. His eyes narrowed. Her skin was so pale, like milk. She nodded, but then she swayed a little, just as she had before, at the end of the *rukbar*.

His chest clutched.

He cursed inwardly. She was going to faint. 'Malik.' His voice cut through the room and

Sariq began to stride quickly, just as Daisy stumbled. Another curse, this one said aloud, and he broke into a run, catching her only a moment before her body crumpled. She would have fallen to the floor if his arms hadn't wrapped around her, lifting her and cradling her against his chest.

The room was silent; he barely noticed. Holding her to him, just as he had when they'd left the tower and she'd been exhausted from the lateness of the hour and the way they'd spent their night, he carried her from the room now, his heart slamming against his ribs in a way that told him all he needed to know.

# CHAPTER THIRTEEN

'PLEASE PUT ME DOWN.'

Such stiffness in her voice, cold and hurt, and he winced inwardly because he understood it. He'd disappeared and he'd hurt her. Pleasure turned to pain, always.

'Sariq? I'm okay. It was just hot and I was tired.'

'You should not have stayed so long.'

He wished condemnation didn't ring through his words but, damn it, didn't she see? Protecting her was important.

She didn't say anything and that was wise. He felt worry and a worry that was close to turning to frustration and anger. Panic, too. A team of men stood outside the doors to her room. 'Where is the doctor?'

'Here, Your Highness.'

At this, Daisy scrambled against him, trying to stand, but he held her tight, pushing through the doors. Only when he reached her bed did he loosen his grip, laying her down on the bed, not wanting to remember the last time he'd done that.

'Please.' Her cheeks were pink. 'This is so silly. I'm fine, really.'

'The doctor will confirm that.' Sariq stepped backwards, allowing the doctor room to move.

He could see Daisy wanted to argue so he played the trump card, which he knew she would listen to. 'Think of the baby, Daisy.'

At that, she stilled and, after a moment, nodded. 'Thank you.' But her gratitude was directed to the doctor. The examination was thorough yet brief. He checked Daisy's blood pressure, heart, temperature, felt the stomach and then listened to the baby's heart using a small handheld device that spilled the noise into the room. And Sariq was frozen to the spot at this small, tangible proof of their child's life. Daisy too lifted her eyes to Sariq's and he saw the emotion in them, the understanding of what they'd done.

Together, they'd made life. It hadn't been planned, and the pregnancy had led to all manner of complications, but it was, nonetheless, a miraculous thing.

'Your blood pressure is a little high, but not alarmingly so. You must rest. Stay hydrated. I'll come back to check on you in an hour.'

'Is that necessary?'

'Yes.' The doctor's smile softened the firmness of his response. 'Absolutely.' He turned to Sariq and bowed, then left.

Sariq stood there for what felt like a very long time, looking at his wife, as the clarity of his situation expanded through his mind. 'Zahrah will sit with you. I'll check on you in the morning.' He stalked towards the door, turned back to look at her as a sinking feeling dropped his stomach to his feet. 'You did well today, Daisy.'

He pulled the door inwards but Daisy was there, moving behind him, grabbing his wrist. 'Don't you dare walk out on me.'

He stared at her, surprise on his features. 'Calm down.'

'No.' And then, she lifted her hands to his chest and pushed him, her expression like fire. 'Damn you, Sariq, stop walking away from me. Can you not even stand to be in the same room with me? Are you worried I'm going to beg you to make love to me again?'

Her anger was so obviously born of hurt. He held her shoulders and lightly guided her from the door, away from the ears of the guards beyond.

'Don't!' She wouldn't be placated.

'I'm not leaving,' he assured her and in that moment he was so desperate to say or do anything that would placate her. 'Just sit down and be calm.'

'I don't want to be calm!'

'For the baby.'

'The baby's fine, you heard the doctor.'

'I heard him say your blood pressure is elevated. Arguing is not going to help that.'

'I don't want to argue with you. I just want you to tell me why you're avoiding me.'

He ground his teeth together, her accusation demanding an answer. But he didn't know what to say—he couldn't frame into words the complexity of his feelings.

'You regret sleeping with me.'

Damn it. He felt caught on the back foot, and it was a new experience, one he didn't like at all. 'It was…unwise.'

'Why?' She thrust her hands onto her hips so even then he was conscious of the jutting of her breasts, the sweetness of her shape, rounded with his baby. What was wrong with him that even in that moment he could want her?

Everything.

That was the problem.

His feelings for Daisy weren't logical. They weren't safe. Nothing about her fitted his usual modus operandi. That was why he had to gain control of this—it was in their mutual interest that he did so.

'I've thought about your request to return to America.' That was true. In the desert, it was all he could focus on. 'That would be unwise and potentially unsafe. I want our child raised here, in Haleth.'

She glowered. 'I'm not asking to go back to America. Not really. I understand why that's not possible.'

He ignored that, continuing with his train of thought as though she hadn't spoken. 'But you do not have to stay here at the palace. There is another palace on the outskirts of the old city. You should move there and live your own life, away from me and the pressures of this royal life.'

She stared at him for several seconds and he had no idea what she was thinking.

'Is that what you want?'

When he thought about what he *wanted*, it was a very dangerous path. So he concentrated instead on what he knew they needed. 'I want our child to be healthy. I want you to be happy. And I want to be able to focus on ruling the RKH, just as I was before.'

'And you can't do that with me here?'

He clenched his jaw, fierce memories burning through him. 'The situation is more complicated than I would like.'

'What does that even mean?'

He expelled a hot sigh. 'You're not like the wife I imagined,' he said, dragging a hand through his hair.

'I'm aware of that.' Her voice was scathing.

Great. He'd offended her once more. 'I mean that we have this history. Even before I knew about your pregnancy, I came to America intending to be with you again. From the moment we met I haven't been able to stop thinking about you. You take up too much space in my brain and I can't have that, Daisy. I can't.'

Her lips parted, her eyes widened, and she was completely still, perhaps replaying his admission.

'You don't want me to leave because you don't like me?'

He frowned. 'Why would you think that?'

'Because you've been ignoring me for a week?'

He was quiet a moment. 'I can't offer you what you need, and it's not fair for me to take what I want from you when I want it—'

'Sex,' she interjected acerbically.

He dipped his head in a silent admission. 'I won't use you like that.'

'So don't use me. Open yourself up to more.'

Her words burst through him, but he was already shaking his head, denying that. 'There's no more. My responsibilities require my full attention.'

'Liar.'

His laugh was a sharp burst. 'I don't think anyone's ever called me that before.'

'Perhaps you've never lied before but you're lying to me now, and to yourself. Why do you think you can't get me out of your head, Sariq? Hmmm?' There was a challenge in her voice, an angry, determined tilt to her chin. 'Why do you think you came to the embassy and propositioned me?'

'Sexual infatuation is one thing,' he said firmly, his tone flat, but she shook her head, dismissing it before he'd even finished.

'If it was sexual infatuation we'd have been sleeping together ever since our marriage. You wanted me, I wanted you. Instead, you've deliberately kept me at arm's length because you're terrified of what this could become. You keep *everyone* at a distance. You have no friends, no family. Malik is the closest person to you and he's a curmudgeonly old man who exists purely to serve you. That's not about your damned duty to Haleth. It's about fear. You don't want to get hurt so you're pushing everyone away. I won't let you do that to me.'

He stared at her, disbelief numbing him. 'You can have no idea what my life is like,' he said, after a moment. 'So do not stand there and judge me, Daisy.'

'I know what your life *could* be like.' She changed tack, her voice lower, softer, working its way into his bloodstream so he had to work hard to hold his course. 'Do you think this is easy for me? I'm terrified! Terrified of telling you how I feel, of opening myself up to you, of opening myself up to yet another disastrous marriage. And yet I'm standing here, saying that I feel—'

'Don't.' He lifted a hand, silencing her. 'Don't say what you cannot take back. I don't want to hear it. I can't. I can't offer you the same, and it will be easier for both of us if we pretend—'

'Coward!' She stamped her foot, and he shifted backwards a little, shocked by her reaction.

'I'm in love with you. There! I've said it! Now what are you going to do? Are you going to admit you love me too? That we fell in love in New York and it's inconvenient and crazy and unpredictable but that doesn't change the fact we're in love? Or are you going to cling to the notion that your life will be better if you stay closed off, completely your own person? Immune from emotional pain but so lonely with it.'

His heart was like a hammer inside him, relentless and powerful. Another challenge, just as she always hit him with. He stared at her, and shook his head slowly, his mind like putty.

Her words threatened to overrun him with joy, but the rational, sensible approach to life he'd fixed on many years earlier was not easy to shake.

'I have never suggested I would love you.'

'Damn it, that's not an answer.' She pushed his chest again, her frustration understandable. 'Tell me you don't love me. Say you'll never love me.'

Say it! Tell her what she needed to hear, if that was how he could put an end to this conversation.

Except he couldn't say those words. Contrary to what she had accused him of, Sariq was not a liar. In fact he was unstintingly honest. 'No.'

Her eyes flared wide.

'I will not talk about you and me in the context of love. That's not what our marriage is predicated on.'

'Yes, it is! You're a fool if you can't see that we fell in love in New York. It's not a one-sided thing. I know, because I've been in a relationship like that and this feels completely different. I believe you love me. And I think you're trying to send me away because love is a complication you're not prepared to deal with.'

A muscle throbbed in his jaw. He stared at her, the stark truth of her words so simple, so right.

'Can't you see how right this is? We could have everything we both want in life. I'm not going to distract you from your responsibilities. I want to help you with them. I want to be your partner in every way.'

'No.' A harsh denial, when his heart was bursting through him, begging him to agree to what she was proposing. But his attitudes were forged from the coal fire of pain and were immovable.

'No? Is that all you've got?'

He glared at her. Damn her fire and spirit. Couldn't she see this wasn't going to work?

'I'm sorry, Daisy. I'm…flattered that you care for me.' She made a scoffing noise. 'But our marriage will work better if we treat it as a business arrangement.'

He began to move to the door but she stalled him with a fierce cry. 'You stop right there.'

He turned to face her, his expression like thunder, matching the strength of his feelings.

'I will not spend the rest of my life in a marriage like you've just described. I should never have agreed to this.'

'But you did, and you're here, and soon our baby will be born.'

'I don't care. If you're telling me our marriage is going to be so cold, then to hell with it. I want a divorce.'

He stared at her, panic strangling him for a

moment, making it difficult to frame a response. 'That's not possible.'

'Oh, don't be so ridiculous. Of course it is. It's not what you *want*, but it's absolutely possible. You'll still have your heir. I'll even raise our child here in the RKH so you can be a part of his or her life. But no way am I going to tie myself to you for the rest of my life knowing you'll never accept that you have feelings for me.'

The ultimatum was like an electrical shock, galvanising him. He stared at her for several moments and then nodded. 'I need to think about that.'

This time, when he left, she didn't try to stop him.

Daisy stared at the closed door with an ache in the region of her heart. She'd done it. She'd laid all her cards on the table and he'd refused to admit he cared for her. She'd been wrong, then. It wasn't love. Not from him, anyway.

And now? He was thinking about granting her a divorce.

God, where had her request come from? Fear? Anger? Had she hoped it would snap him out of his state of denial? That it might wake him up and force him to be brave?

She was trembling all over, the fight knocked out of her by the shock she might get exactly what she'd asked for. Another divorce. Another failed marriage. But this one, so much worse than the first. The idea of not having Sariq in her life in any capacity filled her with a hard lump of pain.

But wasn't it better this way? A lifetime was a long time, and she couldn't see that this would get any easier.

The next day she played the piano Sariq had had brought to the palace the day after she'd arrived. She played Erik Satie because there was a pervasive sadness moving through her and Satie suited that. She played for almost two hours, and didn't hear the door pushing inwards. Nor was she aware of Sariq standing in the door frame, watching her, his eyes running over her as if committing her to memory.

When she finished playing though, he shifted and she turned, her blood pounding through her veins at the sight of him. He wore trousers and a business shirt. She wasn't prepared for that.

'Well?' It was like waiting for the executioner's axe to fall.

He moved towards her, coming to stand by the piano. 'I refuse to keep you here against your will.' His face was grim. 'I was wrong to pressure you into this marriage. I acted on instincts. I panicked. If you were serious about wanting a divorce, I'll grant it.'

Oh, crap. It wasn't what she wanted. But what she needed, he wouldn't give her, so that meant divorce was her only option. 'Fine.' She couldn't meet his eyes. She wanted this over. Like ripping off a plaster.

'You will need to stay in Haleth, as you offered. Once our child is born, we can come to a custody arrangement.'

Was she imagining the emotion in his voice? She didn't know any more. Perhaps her own feelings were so strong, so urgent, that they simply coloured her perception.

She nodded, still not looking at him.

'I apologise to you, from the bottom of my heart.'

Now, her gaze met his, but it hurt too much to hold. The look of pity there was the worst thing. She didn't want him to pity her. She wanted his love.

'I should never have slept with you in Manhattan. I have been selfish this whole time. I hope one day you will forgive me.'

'I can forgive you for almost everything,' she said with a small lift of her chin. 'Manhattan. The embassy. Our marriage. Those were decisions you made because you *felt*.' She pressed a finger into his chest, her eyes like little galaxies.

'Agreeing to divorce me is because you refuse to feel. I don't know if I'll ever get past that.'

'Damn it, Daisy.' He dropped his head then, his forehead to hers, his breathing ragged. 'You ask too much of me.'

'I ask nothing of you,' she corrected. 'Except your heart.' But he wasn't going to give it. Daisy could see that. Slowly, she stood, her fingers finding the keys once more, pressing two together. 'It's a beautiful instrument. Don't make the same mistake your father did—don't shut music from your life once I'm gone.'

Her words chased themselves through his mind for days. They whispered to him overnight, waking him before dawn, they spoke to him at the strangest times. When he was running or working, meeting with foreign politicians. Always that strange parting statement settled around him.

*'Don't make the same mistake your father did.'*

He kept the piano and he went to it often. Every day the sun rose and he went through the motions of his day, just as he had before Daisy. He remained committed to his schedule. He didn't enter her suite of rooms. Nor did he use their adjoining balcony. But the piano he visited. He sat at the stool once, pressed the keys, remembered her fingers in those exact same places, the passion that ran through her.

And he thought about the life she should have been living, and would have been leading had her own plans not been so thoroughly derailed by those who were all too willing to take what they could from her without a second thought for what Daisy needed.

He'd been right to refuse to complicate their marriage. Right to insist he wouldn't use her. How much easier that would have been! To pretend there was hope for them. To sleep with her each night, to fold her into his life only so far as he was willing, but all the while remaining steadfastly committed to his duties as ruler of the RKH.

*'Let me help you.'*

She didn't understand the pressures he lived with. He hadn't been raised to share that burden. Daisy was gone, and he was glad. Not because he wanted her to be anywhere else but because he hoped whatever she thought she felt for him would pass.

Except it wouldn't.

She wasn't like that.

She loved him and she always would.

His gut clenched. Guilt cut through him. He turned away from the piano and stalked to his apartment. Malik was there but Sariq dismissed him quickly. 'Not now.'

Forty sunrises had passed without Daisy. Forty mornings, forty nights, forty days that each seemed to stretch for weeks. Time practically stopped. Only in sleep, when she filled his dreams, did he relax.

He craved sleep. Each day, he longed for it, and all because of Daisy. But it wasn't enough. Forty days after she left, he felt broken enough by missing her to accept that the solution to their marriage wasn't so simple. He couldn't send her away and forget about her.

He wasn't the same as he'd been before. She'd changed him, and he'd never change back. Everything was different now.

Cursing, he strode from his room. 'Malik? The helicopter. Immediately.'

# CHAPTER FOURTEEN

'YOU ARE NOT EATING.'

Daisy regarded Zahrah over her water glass. 'I am.'

'Not like before,' Zahrah chided affectionately. 'When you first came to Haleth you could not get enough of our food.'

Daisy's smile was thin. She had nothing in common with the woman she'd been then. 'I'm eating.'

Zahrah compressed her lips but Daisy was saved from an argument she couldn't be bothered having by the sound of helicopter rotor blades. At the same time, a knock sounded at the door. Zahrah moved to intercept it, and a moment later, returned.

'His Highness is here.'

Daisy's pulse was like a tsunami. She curved a hand over her stomach, her eyes flying wide open, her lips parting in surprise. It had been over a month since she'd left the palace. Their last conversation was painfully formal. He'd spoken to her as though she were a stranger.

Why was he here now? She couldn't bear the idea of another stilted, businesslike interaction.

She stood uneasily, pacing towards the windows where she might get a glimpse of him. But the doors opened and she turned, her flowing turquoise dress blowing in the breeze created by his entrance. And she stood there and stared at him, her face too disobedient to flatten of all expression completely.

Butterflies beat against her and she hated that. She hated how reliably he could stir her to a response when she wanted to feel *nothing* for him.

'What are you doing here?'

There was no point with civility, was there? Perhaps there was, but she couldn't be bothered. She was tired, so tired.

He didn't speak though. He stared at her and with every second that passed, her blood moved faster and harder so that it was almost strangling her with its intensity.

'Your Highness?' It was like waking him from a dream. He straightened, turning to Zahrah, then back to Daisy.

'I'd like to speak to you. Is now a good time?'

She startled. His uncertainty was completely

unusual. 'I'm...yes.' She nodded a little uneasily. 'I suppose so. Zahrah?'

'Yes, Your Highness.' Zahrah bowed low. 'Would you like any refreshments, sir?'

'No.' The word was swift. 'Thank you.'

Zahrah left, and still Sariq didn't move. It unsettled Daisy, so she wiped her hands down her front, drawing his gaze to her belly. In the forty days since she'd left the palace, her bump had 'popped'.

She waited for him to speak but he didn't and the silence was agonising. So eventually, she snapped. 'Please tell me why you're here, Sariq.'

He nodded, moving deeper into the room. 'I came—' He shook his head.

'What is it?'

'I came because...'

Nothing. She ground her teeth together. 'What? Is everything okay?'

Emotion, heavy, obvious emotion, moved on his face. 'No.' So simple. 'It's not.'

Daisy's heart rate doubled. 'Why not?'

He stepped towards her, then froze. 'I came because I couldn't not.'

'You're not making any sense.'

'I know.' His throat shifted as he swallowed. 'I came to apologise, because I cannot live with what I said and I did, with how I made you feel. I came because it occurs to me you're living here believing that I don't love you, that I won't love you, when you were right. I do.' Again he pulled at his hair, shaking his head, his eyes heavy with his emotions.

Daisy couldn't move.

'The night of the ball, when those men were apprehended for what they intended to do to you, I went to see them. I wanted to kill them, Daisy. There was nothing measured or calm in my response. Because of how I feel for you I risked undoing all of my father and grandfather's work and dissolving our entire legal system so I could take my revenge. Even my father didn't do this when my mother was murdered.' He swallowed once more.

Daisy was incapable of speech or movement.

'Loving you terrifies me because there is no limit to what I would do for you if you asked it of me. If anyone hurt so much as a finger on your hand, I would have the kingdom turned upside down until they were found and brought to justice. I'm terrified that I cannot be what my country needs of me when I feel this way for you.'

A strangled noise escaped Daisy's throat.

'But if the last forty days have taught me anything, it's that I cannot live without you either. Perhaps it's the smart thing to do, but I cannot be smart if it means losing you. I won't.' He crossed the room, lifting her face in his palms, staring down at her with such obvious amazement that her heart turned over as though it were being stitched into a new position. 'You are so brave. Fearless and strong, courageous, incredible. You faced up to how you felt about me even after what you've been through. After what *I* put you through. You are generous and good and I pushed at you, just like you said, pushing you away, unable to see a middle ground with you. Perhaps there isn't one. Perhaps loving you will mean I cannot rule as I otherwise might have. I don't care.'

But a sob burst through her. 'I care. I won't have you choose a life with me if you believe it weakens you.' She lifted a hand to his chest though, softening her statement with a gentle touch. 'I have too much faith in you for that.' Her fingers moved gently across the flesh that concealed his heart. 'You didn't kill those men. You stayed within the bounds of the law, because you are a good sheikh and an excellent man. You will rule this kingdom with all your goodness, and I will be at your side, making sure of that. I have no intention of being your weakness, Sariq. I want to be your biggest support and your greatest strength. Understood?'

He groaned, shaking his head. 'How can you

be so good to forgive me after what I put you through?'

She bit down on her lip. 'I didn't say I'd forgiven you.'

His features tightened. 'No, of course not. I misunderstood. I know it will take time for me to make it right between us, but I want to do that, Daisy.'

Her stomach flipped. 'I believe you.'

'And because you are clearly so much wiser than I in these matters, I ask only that you tell me how. What do I do to make amends?'

His hands dropped to her stomach and he closed his eyes, inhaling. 'I want you and our child to be in my life. Please, Daisy.'

And she smiled because she knew he meant it, and because she wanted, more than anything, to grab the dream of this future with both hands.

'Well…' She pretended to think about it. 'Perhaps we should put the divorce on hold. At least while I consider my options.'

He was disappointed, and there was a tiny part of her that enjoyed that. But she couldn't string it out any longer—it was too cruel.

'There are some things you could do to help me with that, you know.'

Hope flicked in his eyes. 'Oh?' Then, more seriously, his voice gruff, 'Anything.'

She lifted a finger to his lips, silencing him.

'Love me.' That was it. Nothing more complex than that.

'I do.'

'Good.' Her smile beamed from her. 'Love me with all your heart, for all your life, and don't ever stop.'

He pulled her against his chest, holding her tight, breathing her in. Their hearts beat in unison. Happiness burst through her.

'Not only is that something I can manage, it turns out it's completely non-negotiable.'

His kiss sealed that promise, and she surrendered to it, to him and to the future she knew they'd lead.

A year later, she stared out at the packed auditorium, anxiety a drum in her soul that was lessened only by the presence in the front row of her husband, the powerful Sheikh Sariq Al Antarah. Since returning to the palace, he'd insisted she further her piano studies. Leaving to attend a school like the Juilliard wasn't possible—once their son Kadir was born, named for his grandfather, she found she didn't want to go anywhere anyway. But Sariq saw no obstacle to that. He engaged world-famous pianists to come to the palace and work with her.

And now, all that effort had culminated in this. A performance that had sold out within minutes, the proceeds of which were going towards the charitable institution she'd established, helping women with mental health issues. Nerves were like fireflies in her veins but she closed her eyes and lifted her hands to the keyboard.

It was a perfect moment with infinite possibilities. She began to play and felt all the hopes of her childhood, the aspirations she'd nurtured for so long, bearing fruit. Who she'd been then, who she was now, unified in one dazzling, magical moment. She smiled, because she was truly happy, and suspected she would be for ever after.

\* \* \* \* \*